Terri picked up the lotion and squirted a mound of the cream into her palm to begin the rubdown.

But when she started to work the lotion into his skin, her hands froze.

Dear God. *This man wasn't Richard!*

The burnished, hard-muscled leg did *not* belong to her ex-husband!

Terri began to tremble. Without hesitation she rushed to his side and bent over him so she could peer into his eyes.

A pain-filled gray gaze stared back at her between dark lashes. There was a frantic urgency in his look she could feel to her bones.

"You poor man," she whispered in a shaky voice. "All this time everyone has thought you were my ex-husband. No wonder you've been so upset."

The man let out a moan, which she took for a yes.

NINE TO FIVE

From boardroom...to bride and groom!

**A secret romance, a forbidden affair,
a thrilling attraction?**

Working side by side, nine to five—and beyond...
No matter how hard these couples try
to keep their relationships strictly professional,
romance is definitely on the agenda!

But will a date in the office diary
lead to an appointment at the altar?
Find out in this exciting new miniseries
from Harlequin Romance®.

Look out for Rebecca's next book,
Bride Fit for a Prince (#3740),
on sale March 2003

THE TYCOON'S PROPOSITION

Rebecca Winters

TORONTO • NEW YORK • LONDON
AMSTERDAM • PARIS • SYDNEY • HAMBURG
STOCKHOLM • ATHENS • TOKYO • MILAN • MADRID
PRAGUE • WARSAW • BUDAPEST • AUCKLAND

ISBN 0-373-03729-5

THE TYCOON'S PROPOSITION

First North American Publication 2002.

Copyright © 2002 by Rebecca Winters.

Visit us at www.eHarlequin.com

Printed in U.S.A.

CHAPTER ONE

"Aren't you going to invite me in?"

Matt Watkins was a nice-looking divorced guy who'd recently moved to Lead, South Dakota, to manage a busy service station.

Tonight had been their first official date, but already Terri Jeppson knew she could never be interested in him. She sensed he was looking for a wife. It would be better to dash his hopes now.

"I'm sorry, Matt. I start work early in the morning and—"

"You're still in love with your ex," he broke in before she could finish, sounding more hurt than angry.

It was on the tip of her tongue to tell him her love for Richard had died an early death during their six-year marriage. But she caught herself in time.

"Maybe I am, and it took going out with someone else to realize it," she said. It was an excuse she felt he could live with. "Please forgive me. I really did have a wonderful time with you tonight. Thank you for dinner and the movie."

He stared hard at her. "When you think you're over him, let me know."

She nodded before shutting her apartment door. Glad the evening had come to an end so she could stop feeling guilty, she walked into the kitchen and automatically turned on her answering machine.

Her job as assistant head of the chamber of commerce meant she received a lot of calls transferred to her apartment after hours. Summer was the busiest time. July was the worst in terms of the swarms of tourists wanting to see Mount Rushmore and vacation in the Black Hills.

While she waited to hear what problems needed trouble-shooting tonight, she sifted through the mail she hadn't bothered to look at earlier.

The first two calls were from her mother and sister Beth who lived in Lead with her husband Tom. Unfortunately Beth had discovered Terri was going out on a date. Her family was so eager for her to meet a man who was "worthy" of her, their interest in her nonexistent love life was transparent. They weren't going to like it when she told them she wouldn't be seeing Matt again.

Another message played. "Mrs. Jeppson?" it began, letting her know it had to do with business. She tossed her junk mail in the wastebasket while she listened.

"My name is Martha Shaw. I'm calling from Creighton Herrick's office at the Herrick Corporation Headquarters in Houston, Texas. Your husband, Richard, was injured in an accident where he's been working. We've been told you should come as quickly as possible. A special family emergency visa has been arranged for you to enter the country."

Country?

"Since this won't require you going into the jungle, you won't need any immunizations. The company will pay for your transportation and hotel. After you hear this message, please phone me at the following number day or night so I can book your flight and make hotel accommodations for you."

Terri stood there in shock.

She and Richard had been divorced for almost a year, and had been separated six months before that. There'd been no communication between them since their divorce had become final. She'd thought he was out of her life forever.

Why would he have lied about his marital status when she knew he was happy to be a free man with no ties?

As for working outside the U.S., she couldn't imagine it unless a glazier could make a lot more money somewhere else.

The whole thing was a complete mystery to her, but whatever the explanation, it appeared his condition was very serious, otherwise the company wouldn't have gotten in touch with her.

After playing back the message so she could write down the phone number, she made the call. It only rang twice before someone picked up.

"Martha Shaw speaking."

"Hello? Ms. Shaw? This is Terri Jeppson."

"Oh, good. I'm glad you got my message."

"Thank you for phoning me. How serious is Richard's condition?"

"I wish I had those particulars, but I don't. I'm sorry. One of the staff from the Herrick office in Ecuador phoned the company here in Houston, informing us that your husband had been hurt."

Ecuador?

"I'm afraid she couldn't give me any specifics, but that's not unusual when the work site is miles from the city center. The message would have been relayed through a variety of people to finally reach us.

"After you arrive in Guayaquil, you're to phone the office there. I'll give you the number before we hang up. By the time you reach Ecuador, I'm sure they'll be able to give you a lot more information and tell you which hospital your husband was taken to. The important thing is to get you down there as quickly as possible."

A few more minutes' conversation and all Terri's travel and hotel arrangements had been made. After thanking Ms.

Shaw, Terri phoned her boss with the news that she had to take emergency leave.

Ray Gladstone, the head of the chamber of commerce, couldn't have been nicer about it. He said he'd handle everything while she was gone and wished her a safe trip down.

Then she called her mother and explained what was happening. As much as her parent had disliked Richard for the years of pain he'd caused, her compassion for his being alone and hurt in a foreign country won out. She told Terri she and Beth would look after the apartment in her absence.

With no time to lose, Terri got busy cleaning and packing, all the while reflecting on what a difference one phone call had made. Ages ago she'd relegated Richard to the past. Now suddenly there seemed to be no choice but to fly down and be with him. As her mother had said, it was the charitable thing to do.

Terri's mind had to stretch back a long way to remember that she'd once been in love with him. Raised in Spearfish, South Dakota, by his aunt and uncle who was a master glazier, Richard had learned the trade well.

It wasn't until after their deaths that he'd landed a glazier's job in Lead where he'd met Terri and they'd married. She hadn't known about his dark side back then.

Little by little it manifested itself as his growing restlessness kept him moving from one work location to another, one state to another. He always wanted more money, a bigger job. She suspected there were other women. He had a drinking problem which he'd tried to hide around her when he came home in-between jobs.

Though she no longer thought about or missed the man who'd been unable to fulfill her as a husband, there was a part of her that would always love the memory of the twenty-two-year-old with the laughing blue eyes who'd asked her to marry him.

As it turned out, he was a man with more charm than substance.

The long separations, his inability to settle down, two devastating miscarriages when he hadn't been home to help her through either one, all contributed to the breakup of their marriage. Somewhere along the way she'd stopped caring.

But none of that mattered now. Not when he was so far away with no aunt or uncle to comfort him.

Eighteen hours later an exhausted Terri arrived in the city of Guayaquil, populated by upwards of eight million people. The dry climate came as a big surprise. She'd expected a wall of humidity.

After checking into her room at the Ecuador Inn, she immediately rang the number Martha Shaw had given her. The receptionist put her through to one person after another. Finally someone came on the line who told her Richard had been taken to San Lorenzo Hospital. That was all the information they had available.

Terri thanked the person before she took a shower and put on a fresh skirt and blouse. At the bank in the lobby she changed some travelers' checks into local money, then caught one of the taxis waiting in front of the hotel.

She'd been to Los Angeles and New York on different vacations, but the evening traffic here presented a completely different kind of chaos. She considered it a miracle to arrive at the hospital in one piece. When she found the floor in question, a Dr. Dominguez met her at the nursing station.

As she introduced herself to the older doctor who was doing his evening rounds, his dark gaze flicked over her face and figure with admiring male interest.

In heavily accented English he said, ''Your husband will

be very happy to see you. According to a local fisherman who brought him into the hospital three days ago, he called for you repeatedly before losing consciousness.

"With no identification on him, I am afraid it took the hospital authorities some time to determine he worked for the Herrick Company."

"Are you saying he's still in a coma?" she asked in alarm, not bothering to correct the doctor about the fact that she was no longer Richard's wife.

"No, no. He awakened at the hospital. His worst problem is his agitation. Now that you have come, he will get the rest he needs."

"Please, doctor—tell me about his condition."

"There's nothing life threatening. He has had the cuts on his face stitched. There are superficial burns on his palms which will soon heal. Once his dislocated shoulder mends, he will be fine. His most painful injury is to his throat. After the accident, he must have swallowed some contaminant in the seawater that made it burn."

"That's horrible."

"Do not worry. The lining is healing nicely, but for the moment it is swollen and he cannot talk. Another few days and the swelling will be gone. Then he will be able to communicate the same as before and tell us exactly what happened to him.

"In the meantime we have swathed his face and head to protect the dressings over the stitches. He was fortunate that the cuts were at the hairline and just beneath the chin, so there will be no disfigurement.

"Depending on a number of factors, he might wish to have some minor plastic surgery done later to the scar below his chin, but I am not sure that will be necessary."

"May I see him now?"

"Certainly. Keep in mind we've left the overhead light off in his room to help him rest."

Terri nodded.

''Sister Angelica will take you to him.'' He turned and spoke in rapid Spanish to the nun who led Terri down the hall to her ex-husband's hospital room.

Terri had always been frightened of mummies, so when she peered inside and saw what looked like a mummy's head and torso extending beyond the sheet, she let out an involuntary cry.

His head moved a trifle in Terri's direction. The sister in her white habit put a finger to her lips as if to warn Terri not to let her emotions disturb their patient again.

Ashamed of her outburst, she nodded to the sister, then moved to the side of the bed.

His right arm was in a sling. There were needles in both arms above the wrists. As for his hands, they looked like they'd been fitted with little white gauze mitts. An oxygen mask covered the nose opening. Just looking at him made her feel as if she was going to suffocate.

''Richard?'' she said in a soft voice. ''It's Terri. I flew down here as soon as I was told about the accident.''

She heard a funny little sound come out of him.

''No—don't try to talk. The doctor said your throat will heal faster if you don't use your vocal cords. I'm here now and I'll sit with you as long as you want me to.''

Reaching for the chair, she placed it near the IV stand and sat down. The sister smiled approvingly before leaving the room.

Richard had played football in high school and was six feet of sturdy muscle. With all the bandages, he looked even bigger. A portion of his uninjured left shoulder was the only part of his body she could really see in the dim wall light.

Normally he worked with a shirt on, but she guessed it must have made him feel more macho to take it off. That would explain the bronzelike tan built up over months of exposure under a hot sun.

He made another muffled sound. She watched him lift his left hand from the sheet.

For a man who'd always been so restless both within and without, his suffering had to be extreme. She leaned forward and gently patted his lower leg draped by the sheet.

''The doctor said you're going to be fine. He thinks any scarring will be so slight, you might not even have to undergo minor plastic surgery. That's a blessing. You always were a heartthrob.''

She watched his legs stir beneath the sheet. No doubt he was in unbearable pain.

It was bad enough that they hadn't lived together for at least a year and a half. But to have to meet her former husband under these precarious circumstances made their meeting even more difficult. What did she say to the man who was a virtual stranger to her at this point?

''Dr. Dominguez told me you called out my name several times to the fisherman who saved you. I have to admit it surprised me to learn that you'd listed me as your spouse on your work application.

''I can't imagine why you did that when we're divorced. I happen to know you wanted it as much as I did. But I'm not sorry to be here. You shouldn't be alone at a time like this. My family sends their best wishes. They want you to get well as soon as possible, too.''

He lifted his left arm once more and brushed it against her arm before lowering it again. Perhaps it was his way of thanking her for coming. She didn't really know.

''As soon as the Herrick Corporation notified me, I took emergency leave from the chamber of commerce to fly here. Ray told me not to worry about anything. He said he hoped you'd have a swift recovery.''

While she tried to think of things to say, her heart went out to him for his helpless state.

"I didn't realize you'd taken a job in South America. Judging by your tan, it looks like you've been here quite a while. According to the doctor, you'll be able to talk in a few days. Then you can tell me what you need.

"If there are friends you want me to contact, a woman you've been seeing, I'll do whatever I can to help you get in touch with them."

He made another sound in his throat and tried to lift his head. If anything, she felt as if her presence were disturbing him rather than bringing him a measure of peace.

Afraid to do something wrong that might delay his recovery, she got to her feet.

"You need to rest, Richard. I'm going to go now, but I promise I'll be back in the morning. I'm staying at the Ecuador Inn and will leave my room number in case the hospital needs to get in touch with me about you before tomorrow."

At that moment he moaned more distinctly than before. Worried over his reaction, she hurried from the room and rushed down the hall to the nursing station.

A minute passed before she saw the doctor come out of one of another patient's room. He headed in her direction.

"Leaving so soon?"

"Richard seemed to be more unsettled with me there. He kept trying to talk."

"It is the excitement of seeing his beautiful wife again."

Hardly. If that were the case, there would never have been a divorce.

"Knowing you are here will hasten his recovery," the other man continued.

She shook her head. "Dr. Dominguez? You don't understand. I'm not his wife." It was best he know the truth.

The announcement brought him up short.

"We were divorced eleven months ago," she went on to explain. "Since then I've had no contact with him. I didn't know anything of his whereabouts until the Herrick Corporation got in touch with me.

"Frankly I have no idea why he claimed to be married on his work application. When he's recovered enough to talk, I'm sure he'll explain. What's important to me is that he gets well. But he keeps trying to say something to me, which couldn't be good for his throat.

"I told him I'd be back in the morning. I'm staying at the Ecuador Inn, room 137. You can reach me there, no matter the hour."

"Very good," he murmured, clearly puzzled by the news.

"Doctor? Is he getting enough pain relief?"

"As much as he can tolerate. Perhaps his increased restlessness has been brought on because your presence is a reminder of your broken marriage. Maybe he regrets the divorce and that is the reason why he still claims to be married.

"Sometimes it takes losing something of great value for a man to realize what is really important after all. Have you considered this might be an opportunity for a reconciliation?"

Terri could see where the doctor was going with this, but he would be wrong about the whole situation. Richard wasn't having second thoughts. There was an entirely different reason why he'd claimed to still be married when he'd accepted a job down here.

As for Terri, she couldn't resurrect feelings that had been burned out of her. "Dr. Dominguez? Our marriage was over a long time ago. However I still care for him and want him to recover as soon as possible."

"I want that, too."

"Then I'll see you tomorrow."

She left the floor and took the elevator to the foyer where she asked the receptionist to summon a taxi.

Once back in her hotel room, she rang for room service and ordered dinner. When it arrived, she changed into her nightgown and ate in bed while she talked to her mother and Beth, updating them on Richard's condition.

Beth suggested Richard might have lied because it was the only way he could get the job. Maybe the Herrick Corporation had a rule about their employees being married if they wanted to work outside the U.S.

It was a possibility Terri hadn't thought of. Tomorrow she would visit Richard again, then go to the Herrick office and ask more questions. Right now what she craved was a good night's sleep so she'd be better prepared to deal with the situation in the morning.

But even though she was exhausted, it was hard to settle down. She turned on the television and watched several news programs in Spanish. With the help of her high school Spanish, she was able to figure out some of it. Then she switched to a movie dubbed in Spanish she'd already seen in English, and promptly fell asleep. The television was still on when she awakened at nine the next morning.

Once she'd eaten breakfast in her room, she showered and dressed in another blouse and skirt. After she was ready, she left the hotel and climbed into one of the many taxis waiting out front.

To her delight the temperature outside the hotel wasn't as high as she would have supposed for July. In fact it felt much better here than in Atlanta where she'd changed planes.

On her way to the hospital, she looked around to get better oriented. Guayaquil was a large South American port city. Its proximity to the ocean, plus the masses of dark haired people speaking Spanish made it a fascinating place to be. With so many beautiful women, she imagined

Richard had been enjoying himself here. How sad to think he'd met with an accident that had almost cost him his life.

She knew he liked to fish. Maybe he'd been out in a small boat with his spinning rod when it had happened. Had he gone alone? Was anyone else hurt?

Terri was impatient for answers. But she would have to wait until his throat was healed enough to supply her with details.

Hoping they'd given him something to help him sleep so he'd had a restful night, she hurried down the hospital corridor to his room. The door was ajar. When she peeked inside, she saw a younger doctor standing at the side of the bed unraveling the bandage that was wrapped around Richard's forehead.

He flashed her a broad smile. "Come in, Señora Jeppson. I'm Dr. Fortuna. We have been expecting you."

She did his bidding. Evidently Dr. Dominguez hadn't informed the staff about Richard's divorced status yet. "If your husband could talk, I'm sure he would tell you he is glad you are here. I have been checking his stitches. The cut under his chin shows no infection."

At that news, Terri was relieved. She sank down in the chair to watch. The bed had been raised so Richard was sitting up. His oxygen mask had been removed.

In a minute she saw the top of his head. He'd always worn his dark hair marine style, very closely cropped. Since he'd been in South America, it appeared he'd let it grow. She could tell it was at least an inch or two longer now. Maybe even more.

"Ah," the doctor murmured with satisfaction as he removed the dressing. "Everything looks very good. No one would guess you had a cut there. Stay still while I put on a new dressing. If there's no infection by tomorrow, you won't have to wear the head wrap anymore."

Just hearing those words helped Terri to breathe a little easier. She could imagine Richard felt equally relieved. Confined like that, he had to be going out of his mind. In fact he would probably have ripped off the bandages by now if he'd been able to get at the gauze.

"What about his burns, Doctor?"

"They are much better. Tomorrow we will unwrap his hands and apply a dressing which will free his fingers. I am happy to say that he is breathing at ninety-five perfect capacity and no longer needs oxygen."

Thank goodness for that. "What about his shoulder?"

"It was an anterior dislocation which is the most common. The surgeon performed a reduction. All your husband has to do now is wear this sling for three or four weeks and he will be fine. To his credit, he is in remarkable shape. Has he always worked out?"

Richard?

"Not since he played football in high school."

"Then he has been keeping a secret from you. You do not stay this solid without help."

Maybe he'd been going to a gym for the last eighteen months. She had no idea.

"Is his throat really going to get better?"

"In a few days it will be like new."

"I'm sorry I sound so impatient."

"That's a wife's prerogative."

Ignoring his comment she said, "I wish there were something I could do for him right now."

The doctor finished rewrapping his patient's head, then lowered the bed so Richard was lying almost flat.

"I can think of one thing."

"What?"

"You could give his legs and feet a soothing massage with that lotion over on the table. It will relax his whole body and help him to sleep."

"I'll do it."

"Excellent. I am sure your husband is looking forward to such a lovely wife ministering to his needs."

The doctor was mistaken on that score, but she was equally certain Richard craved any relief from the pain that he could get. If a massage would help, she was only too glad to provide it.

"Tomorrow we will put him in the shower for the first time. That will make him feel really good, too."

Terri had no doubt of it and thanked him.

"I'm impressed with the wonderful care you're getting," she said after the doctor had left the room. "Tomorrow you'll be stripped of all these bandages. I know you can't wait. Until then I'll do as he suggested and try to bring you some comfort."

She moved over to the table and picked up the lotion, and then walked to the end of the bed. After pulling out the sheet to expose his left leg to the knee, she squirted a mound of the cream in her palm to begin the rubdown.

But when she started to work the lotion into his skin, her hands froze.

Dear God.

This man wasn't Richard!

The burnished, hard-muscled leg did *not* belong to her ex-husband! Richard's legs were shorter, bulkier, hairier; his foot was wider, not as long.

Terri began to tremble. She removed her hands and hurried to the door to turn on the overhead light.

Without hesitation she rushed to his side and bent over him so she could peer into his eyes.

Pain-filled gray eyes stared back at her between dark lashes. There was a frantic urgency in his look she could feel to her bones.

"You poor man," she whispered in a shaky voice. "All

this time everyone has thought you were my ex-husband. No wonder you've been so upset.''

He let out a moan which she took for a yes.

Her eyes filled with tears. ''I'm sorry it took me this long to discover the truth. Last evening when I arrived, Dr. Dominguez told me they were keeping the light off in here so you could sleep. If I'd been able to look into your eyes, I would have known immediately you weren't Richard.

''The fisherman who brought you in said you called out my name. That means you knew Richard. I assume you were friends or colleagues. Were you both in the accident?''

The stranger lifted his head enough to nod, but it was clearly a strain. Nevertheless it meant he understood her English.

''Lie still,'' she begged. ''Please don't exert yourself. Obviously you have family and friends looking for you. They must be in agony wondering where you are.

''I'll alert the staff right now, then I'll leave and go straight to the police to find out if the Herrick company or someone else has put out a missing persons report for you. I suppose it's possible Richard was taken to another hospital in the city.''

This time the stranger shook his head.

She was trying to understand. ''If he's not at a hospital, do you know where he is?''

He nodded again, but the strain on him had taken its toll. His eyelids closed. The unidentified man had to be in grueling pain. She could feel it.

''That's all right. You sleep while I'm gone. I swear I'll be back as soon as I can.''

She covered his leg and tucked the sheet in place. Then she put the lotion on the table. After turning off the light, she grabbed her purse and tore out of the room.

To her relief the same doctor happened to be at the nursing station down the hall. She took him aside and told him what she'd discovered. He looked shocked and said he'd immediately notify the staff as well as the head of the hospital.

Within a half hour she'd told the same story to Captain Ortiz, an officer at the main police station in Guayaquil. He knew nothing about an accident at sea and proceeded to ask a lot of questions. She gave him a full description of her ex-husband. As for the stranger lying in the hospital bed, there was less to tell about him.

The captain said he would send another officer to the hospital to interview the doctors who were taking care of him. If the police could find the fisherman who'd brought him in, it would answer a lot of questions. At some point he would get back to her either at the hospital or the hotel.

Terri in turn said she would find out where her ex-husband was living. The bandaged stranger had indicated that Richard wasn't in a hospital. That had to mean he hadn't been badly hurt in the accident and was convalescing at his apartment or wherever it was that he lived. If she found him first, she would phone the captain right away. He agreed that it sounded like the best plan of action.

After agreeing to stay in close touch, Terri left the police station for the Herrick head office. The taxi driver knew the name and drove her to the heart of the city where he deposited her in front of a complex of buildings, one of which housed the company in question.

A Latin beauty sat at the main reception. When Terri told her she needed some information about one of the employees who worked for the Herrick Corporation, the woman told her she couldn't give out confidential information.

However as soon as Terri mentioned Martha Shaw, Mr.

Creighton Herrick's secretary, her tone changed. The woman made a quick phone call before looking up Richard's record on the computer. She gave Terri his address, but there was no phone number listed.

After thanking the receptionist, Terri asked her to call for a taxi. Once that was done, she went outside to wait.

When the driver pulled up in front and she showed him the address, he told her it was located twenty-five miles south of the city and would take close to an hour to get there.

Terri didn't care about that. She climbed in the back seat and handed him fifty dollars to cover the round-trip. Then she told him to step on it.

He smiled before starting up the taxi to merge with the other cars. The drive turned out to take fifty minutes in the early-afternoon traffic. By the time they reached the city limits, she could tell that the barrios in the outskirts were more run-down.

Eventually he pulled up in front of a small three-story apartment called the Mirador. There was no landscaping to speak of, and a cluster of little children played on the stairs. She asked him to stay put while she went to the door. In case Richard wasn't there, she needed to be sure she had a ride back into town.

The driver nodded and reached for a magazine to read.

Number ten put Richard on the second floor. She stepped past the curious children to find his apartment, then knocked. When there was no answer she knocked again.

"Richard?" she called out. "It's Terri. If you can hear me, let me know. I heard about the accident and have flown all this way to see you."

Still nothing.

Afraid he could be inside unable to get up and answer

the door, she turned the handle, hoping he might have left it unlocked.

"*Aiyee!*" she heard a woman scream.

Terri didn't know who was more frightened.

Through the opening in the door, which the chain guard allowed, she saw a woman probably much younger than Terri's twenty-seven years. With long black hair and liquid-brown eyes, Terri could well understand her ex-husband's attraction.

The woman stood there wearing Richard's yellow robe, looking very pretty and very pregnant.

CHAPTER TWO

"*BUENOS tardes.*" Terri spoke first. "*Habla Ingles?*"

The other woman shook her head without the slightest hint of welcome in her expression.

At this point Terri had only her two years of Spanish to rely on. "*Por favor, donde esta Richard?*" Heavens! It had been so long since high school, she couldn't remember if she was supposed to use Estar or Ser.

The woman responded too fast. Terri couldn't follow.

She tried again. "*Quiero hablar con Richard.*"

There was another spate of unintelligible words before the woman shut the door in Terri's face.

If Richard had been inside, Terri was positive he would have come out to see what was going on.

The fact that his lover seemed to be angry rather than in despair, led Terri to believe Richard had to be all right. In fact, the fiery woman was probably expecting him home later in the day and couldn't believe some strange American woman had appeared at the door unannounced and unwanted.

Only jealousy could have prompted her to behave in such a rude manner. It was more than possible Richard had never told this woman about Terri. Certainly he'd never expected to see his ex-wife again. Especially not down here in Guayaquil, which was about as far from Lead, South Dakota, as you could get.

Terri hurried back to the taxi and they left for the city. En route she asked the driver to drop her off at an upscale department store near the San Lorenzo Hospital. She needed to make a few purchases.

Assuming for the moment Richard was out of danger, Terri's thoughts converged on the stranger who'd been lying in a hospital bed since he'd been rescued. The painful desperation in his beautiful gray eyes would haunt her for a long time to come.

How frightening it must have been to wake up in an unfamiliar place, unable to talk while everyone around him thought he was someone else!

He probably had a wife who was out of her mind with grief because he was missing. Until a relative or friend came to claim him, Terri would stay with him and encourage him to get better. It was the least she could do.

An hour and a half later she rushed inside the hospital with her arms loaded. After taking the elevator, she hurried down the hall of his floor where various helpers were serving dinner to the patients who could eat.

She stopped at the nursing station long enough to be offered a tray of food for herself, then she breezed into his room with her packages.

"Hi!" she called out in a soft voice, not wanting to jar him. As he lifted his left hand in greeting, her dinner arrived. She put everything down on the floor, then reached for the tray and drew the chair next to him so she could be seated.

"I was gone a lot longer than I'd intended. First off I went to the police station and explained the situation. Then I took a taxi to the Herrick office. I've been so busy I haven't eaten anything since breakfast. Now I'm starving.

"I hope you don't mind my eating in front of you. If the smell makes you nauseous, put up your hand and I'll eat out in the hall."

He made no gesture, so she had to believe it was all right.

"Earlier when you told me you knew where Richard was, I asked the receptionist at the Herrick office to give me his address. It took a little doing, but she finally complied. From there I took another taxi out to his apartment to see if he was there, and found a woman in residence. Judging by her pregnant condition, it seems Richard's been living with her for a long time.''

More indecipherable sounds came out of the stranger.

''She wasn't in the least happy to see *me* at the door. I tried out my Spanish on her, but she spoke too fast for me to understand. Later I'll try to get in touch with Richard through someone at the office who knows him personally. In the meantime, I'm anxious to help you in any way I can.''

The chicken and beans tasted good. So did the fruit juice which was an interesting blend of peach and something else, maybe mango.

After she'd drained the glass she said, ''There's a Captain Ortiz at the police station who's working on your case. He hadn't heard of any accident at sea. However with the information I've given him, he said he'll come up with some answers soon and hopefully find out who you are.

''If we don't hear from him in the next few hours, I'll call him before I leave. In case there's no news, I have an idea.

''Since the doctor said they'd be removing the bandages on your hands in the morning, maybe with my help you could write your name or your home phone number on a piece of paper. That is, if it doesn't hurt too much.

''Depending on your mobility, you might even be able to write down a word that will tell me Richard's location. One way or another we'll unravel this mystery.''

She finished the rest of her chicken, then put the tray over on the table. Eager to do something to bring a little pleasure to the man who'd been through so much suffering, she turned to him.

"Now that I've eaten, I'll give your legs that massage you've been waiting for."

Not expecting an answer from the stranger, she picked up the lotion and walked over to the bed.

After squeezing lotion up and down his left leg, she began to rub it in. "When I was in junior high, we once read *The Invisible Man* for Halloween. That's a holiday in the States, in case you haven't heard of it. The children dress up in costumes and go door to door asking for candy.

"Anyway, there was this scientist who'd made himself invisible. He wrapped himself in bandages so it would outline his body. But sometimes a dog or a cat would chase after him in the streets and pull the bandages away. People would scream in terror when they couldn't see anything underneath.

"It was a really fascinating concept. Of course I love science fiction of all kinds, so the story captured my attention right off. Anyway, when I walked in this room yesterday and saw you, I was reminded of that story.

"Thank goodness when I looked in your eyes this morning, I saw life there staring back at me," she teased. "You're kind of a cross between him and *The Mummy*.

"Maybe you don't know about this old movie. It concerns a guard of the Pharaoh who dared to love his Egyptian queen. For his punishment the other guards turned him into a living mummy. It still gives me chills just thinking about it."

A faint noise came out of him. It could mean most anything.

"If your feet are ticklish, I'm sorry. I'll try not to drive you crazy."

When she'd finished with one leg, she moved around the end of the bed and started on the other. Strange how it felt so natural doing this small service for a total stranger. The darkness of the room with just the two of them added a certain intimacy, which she enjoyed.

In truth it was much easier than if it had been Richard lying here. Too much unhappy history had passed between them to have made it an enjoyable experience.

"Do you know? I haven't the faintest idea of your nationality. Obviously you understand English, but you could be from so many different countries besides Ecuador, your predicament has fueled my imagination.

"You've probably never been to South Dakota. That's where I live in the States. A small town called Lead, gateway to the Black Hills and Mount Rushmore. Fresh out of college with an English degree, I started working for the local chamber of commerce.

"In the beginning it was only supposed to be a temporary job until I found a good teaching position. However the work became so interesting to me, I've been with them ever since.

"If you asked me what I actually do there, the answer would be a little bit of everything under the sun. Something's always going wrong and I have to fix it. That's why I like it so much.

"Of course my family is there. My mom and my sister Beth who married Tom three months ago. Now they're expecting a baby. You already know my marriage to Richard failed, so that's about it. The story of my life. No doubt I've bored you to tears."

She gave his foot a final rub, then covered his legs with the sheet. "Since there's no television in here, I'll read you what's on the front page of today's newspaper. Someone left it in the room. In case you're a native Spanish speaker, please forgive my pronunciation."

Terri washed her hands, then put on some lotion from her own purse before placing the chair near the wall light so she could read the print.

"This is from *El Telegrafo*. Let's see...

"*Mediante oficio No. 19370 enviado al Presidente del Congreso, José Cordero Acosta, el Procurador General del Estado, Ramón Jiménez Carbo, señala que su pronunciamiento sobre la inconstitucionalidad del artículo 33 del Reglamento que dispuso la prisión domiciliaria para—entre otros—los ex presidentes y ex vicepresidentes de la República, 'tiene carácter vinculante.'*"

She put the paper down. "If I knew what *vinculante* meant, this article would make a lot more sense. But I don't think it would be of interest to anyone who isn't involved in local politics. Of course, maybe you are. If so, forgive me if I don't read further."

To her surprise, his body appeared to be shaking. Alarmed, she jumped up from the chair and hurried over to his side.

"What's wrong? Do you need the doctor?"

He shook his head.

"Are you cold?"

Again he made the same gesture.

After a moment of consideration, "Are you laughing?"

He nodded.

Her lips curved into a smile. "My Spanish was that awful?"

Once more he shook his head.

"Liar," she whispered, loving their one-sided conversation more than she'd loved anything in years.

"I'm glad you can laugh, but maybe you shouldn't, just in case it pulls at the stitches under your chin. When your wife comes rushing in, I'm sure she'll be looking for the same attractive man she married before the accident."

He shook his head.

"Don't be modest. I've seen your eyes, remember? And you've got great legs."

His body shook again.

"With that head of dark hair, something tells me there's a real hunk hidden under all those bandages. In case you haven't heard the word 'hunk' before, it means, a good-looking man. In Spanish a woman would say, *muy guapo*. You've probably been called that a lot around here."

She left him long enough to find the packages she'd bought and had asked to be gift-wrapped.

"These are for you. I think they'll fit. You're probably six feet two or three. I thought you'd want to be wearing something more spectacular than a hospital gown when your family shows up."

Terri put the packages on the chair and opened them one at a time. "I bought you these navy pajamas and matching robe. I'm sorry if they're not your taste, but with that tan I think you'll look sensational in them.

"I also picked up these leather sandals. They'll fit a size eleven or twelve foot. In case that sizing doesn't mean anything to you, be assured you'll be able to wear them."

She held everything up for him to see. "After your shower in the morning, you can put these on. It will make you feel more normal."

Leaving everything on the chair, she moved it against the wall, then returned to his side.

"I'm sorry Captain Ortiz hasn't phoned yet. I know he would have if there'd been any news. Please don't be disheartened. Who knows? When morning comes, I might walk in here and discover you've got a room full of company.

"In that case, you're going to need a good night's sleep so I think I'd better leave. It's getting late."

He let out another strange sound and shook his mummy-like head.

"What's wrong? You don't want me to go yet?"

Again, his head moved back and forth.

"So—you want me to help you pass the time, is that it?"

His definite nod secretly pleased her. It meant her presence brought him some comfort. It felt good to be needed.

"Since your hearing hasn't been affected, I guess I could stay for a while longer and talk to you. But don't be surprised if one of the sisters comes around to check your vital signs and throws me out. I'll put your new clothes in the drawer so I can sit next to you."

In a few seconds she was seated at his side once more.

"I've just thought of another idea. When my sister and I were little girls, we used to print the names of movie stars on each other's backs and try to guess who they were. The one who got the most right answers on the first round had to buy the other one a treat the next day.

"Why don't I try printing a continent on your leg? The one you come from. You nod when I've stumbled onto it."

Excited over her own idea, she uncovered his leg and started drawing the letters for Europe up his shin bone.

When she'd finished, his head remained motionless.

"Hmm. How about this?"

She wrote South America.

Still there was no gesture from him.

Next she printed the words North America.

Now she got the nod she'd been waiting for.

"American?"

Another emphatic nod.

Terri shot to her feet. "I should have played this game with you earlier." Her voice shook. "Do you work for the Herrick Company, too?"

He gave her a nod.

She sucked in her breath. "Okay. Let's learn your first name. I'll start saying the alphabet. You lift your right hand slightly when I come to the right letter. *A*," she began. "*B*."

He lifted his hand.

"Second letter. *A. B. C. D. E.*"

Again, his hand moved.

She went through the alphabet a third time. When she reached *N*, he raised his hand.

"Your name is Ben!" she cried out. "Short for Benjamin?"

He nodded.

With her heart racing she said, "Let's do your last name." She went through the same process. It seemed his last name started with an *H*. By the time she'd been through the alphabet seven times, he'd spelled the name Herrick.

Terri blinked. "Is it a coincidence you have the same name as the company you work for?"

He shook his head.

"You mean you're the head of the company here?"

Contact at last!

Ben nodded as he gazed into her expressive eyes. They widened in incredulity. Their heavenly blue color reminded him of Texas bluebonnets which flowered every spring at the ranch.

With her dark-blond hair cut in a kind of windswept shag, and a mouth shaped like a heart when she was pondering something serious, she looked utterly adorable to him.

"But if that's true, how is it possible no one's looking for you of all people? Captain Ortiz never said anything about the head of your company disappearing. It doesn't make sense! But that doesn't matter right now. The important thing is that you're alive and on the road to recovery."

He watched helplessly as she bit the soft underside of her lip. What he'd give to taste such an enticing mouth.

"I'll call Martha Shaw and tell her you're here so she can let your family know."

No! Lord, no. Not Martha.

He moaned, then lifted his hand in the air. Unfortunately his blond angel of mercy wasn't paying any attention to him.

Stunned over her discovery, Terri grabbed for her purse to get the secretary's number. When she found the paper she'd written it on, she hurried over to the wall phone at the head of the bed.

Using her phone card, she made the call. This time it took six rings before the other woman answered.

"Martha Shaw speaking."

"Ms. Shaw? This is Terri Jeppson."

"Yes, Terri. How is your husband?"

"I believe he's all right, but I haven't seen him yet. There's another reason I'm calling." She struggled for breath.

"You sound upset. What's wrong?"

"The man the hospital thought was my husband has turned out to be someone else. The trouble is, his throat was burned and he can't talk. However I discovered a way to communicate with him. He says his name is Benjamin Herrick."

After a long silence, "*Ben* is the patient?" She sounded as shaken as Terri.

"Yes. I need to inform the police, but I thought you should be told first so you can get in touch with his family and co-workers. Naturally he's had no visitors.

"The thing is, today's his fourth day in here. Though he's been getting excellent treatment, it has to have been a ghastly experience for him not being able to talk or explain who he really was."

Ben heard the tremor in Terri Jeppson's appealing voice. The woman's compassion for his plight—never mind the fact that she was still waiting for word about her ex-husband—touched him in places he hadn't known existed.

"How bad is he?" Martha asked in a pain-filled whisper. "Don't spare me."

Terri's hand tightened on the receiver. The other woman sounded like she'd taken the news personally, almost as if...

"Actually the doctors have assured me he's going to be fine." Without hesitation she told the secretary everything Dr. Fortuna had related to her.

"Thank God he wasn't killed. I'll let his family know at once."

"Tell them he's at San Lorenzo Hospital, Room W621. There's no use anyone phoning his room. He won't be able to use his voice for several more days. But I'm sure either Dr. Dominguez or Dr. Fortuna will be happy to discuss his condition if the family will call the sixth floor nursing station."

"I'll convey the message. Terri?" There was a hint of pleading in her tone. "Would you put the phone to Ben's ear so I can say something to him before we hang up?"

The woman was in love with him. Terri could hear it in her voice.

"Yes. Of course."

She turned in his direction.

"Mr. Herrick?"

Ben groaned. Now that Terri knew his identity, he could tell she no longer felt as free to treat him the way she had earlier when she'd believed he was alone in the world and lost... *Damn* the situation.

"Ms. Shaw wants to say something to you."

Bile rose in his throat. Martha had no shame. She would use anyone to get what she wanted, but there wasn't anything he could do about the situation right now. He nodded to Terri.

With great care she placed the hearing end of the receiver next to his ear and left it there. He saw how she purposely looked away from his eyes to give him some privacy. She did everything right. He was utterly charmed by her.

"Ben? I hope you can hear me. It's Martha! Thank God you're all right!" she cried in a tear-filled voice. "I've been trying to reach you for a week at least. When you didn't return my calls, I knew something was wrong. But I thought it was because you were angry over the letter I wrote you a while ago."

Repulsed would be a better word.

"As soon as we hang up, I'll tell Creighton so he can phone your parents. When they hear what's happened, they'll be down to bring you back to Houston for a recuperation period. I'd give anything in the world to do it myself, but I know I don't have that right. At least not yet."

Yet?

"Oh, Ben," she whispered emotionally. "I can't wait to see you. It's been so long. I know what a terrible mistake I made, but don't you think I've been punished long enough?"

Her tears were wasted on Ben who'd become conscious of the wonderful peach scent coming from Terri's hand as she held the phone close to his ear.

Those soft, feminine hands had brought his body so much pleasure, the endorphins they'd produced had blotted out any pain he'd been feeling. He'd never wanted her to stop.

"Please, Ben—when we see each other again, tell me we can work things out. I've always been in love with you. You know it's true! There's so much I want to say to you.''

Ben couldn't get rid of Martha fast enough. Frustrated as hell, he lifted his left hand so Terri would realize he wanted her to hang up the phone. He had information to give her about her ex-husband.

Terrie saw his left arm go up. She imagined Ms. Shaw had said what she'd wanted to say.

Putting the phone to her own ear she said, "Ms. Shaw?"

"I wasn't finished talking," the other woman snapped.

"I'm sorry, but Mr. Herrick signaled me that he was tired. Perhaps if you waited until tomorrow to call again, he'll have more strength.''

Ben nodded, letting Terri know she'd said the right thing.

"Do you think he heard me?'' There was that pleading sound in Martha's voice again. Something was going on here, but it wasn't any of Terri's business.

"Yes, of course.''

"Thank you for phoning me, Terri. I'll inform everyone who needs to know. Please don't hesitate to call if there's any help you require with your travel plans. I hope everything's all right with your husband.''

"Me, too. Goodbye, Ms. Shaw.''

She hung up the phone before walking around the other side of the bed to the table where she'd left her purse.

Mr. Herrick made a couple of sounds. If she didn't miss her guess, he didn't want her to go yet. She rushed over to his side.

"I have to get back to the hotel and phone Captain Ortiz.''

To her surprise he gave an emphatic shake of his head. Even bandaged to the hilt and out of commission, she felt his aura of authority.

"You've had enough excitement for one evening and

need your rest now.'' She put his new clothes back out on the chair so they'd be seen by the help. ''I'll tell the nursing staff who you are and leave Ms. Shaw's number with them. Sleep well, Mr. Herrick.''

Don't go, dammit.

He was still making sounds of frustration as she left the room.

Much as she would have loved to stay, she didn't dare. She'd been enjoying their association far too much. In truth, she felt a bond with him that defied logic. It had happened when she'd first looked into his eyes and felt his soul reaching out to her.

Her heart whispered it would be better if she didn't remain in his presence any longer. Otherwise she might crave it more and more. Something told her *that* was a no-no.

Surely a wise woman would walk away right this minute before she learned the answers to burning questions like, did he have a wife? If so, did she know his secretary was in love with him? Was he a womanizer like Richard?

The thought that this man was anything like her ex-husband left Terri feeling strangely desolate. That's why she had to get out of his room and far away from the hospital.

Nothing about this situation had anything to do with her. There was no reason for her to visit him again. She'd done everything she could for Mr. Herrick. By tomorrow morning, he'd be receiving a surfeit of attention from the people who loved him.

The intrigue was over. Mystery solved.

As for Terri, she'd go to the place where Richard worked and see for herself that he was faring all right since his accident. Once that was accomplished, she'd fly home to Lead.

Poor Ray. She'd dumped all her work in his lap. He'd be happy to see her back on the job.

After leaving the information at the nursing station, she left the hospital and took a taxi to the hotel. When she reached her room, the first thing she did was call Captain Ortiz, but he'd turned on his voice mail.

She gave him the news about Mr. Herrick, then related a brief account of her futile attempt to find Richard at his apartment. If the captain had any information concerning her ex-husband's whereabouts, would he please call her at the hotel, no matter the hour?

Having made the call, she hung up the receiver and got ready for bed. Before she fell asleep she phoned Beth and told her the latest developments. Her private thoughts and feelings about Mr. Herrick she kept to herself.

After asking her sister to tell their mother she'd be home within twenty-four hours, Terri hung up.

Afraid her mind would dwell on the man lying in the hospital bed, she pulled out a new bestseller she'd brought with her. But she couldn't get into it. Finally she turned on the television and found another movie to help her fall asleep.

It worked. She didn't waken until she heard the phone ring at eight-thirty the next morning. Reaching for the receiver, she said hello.

"Señora Jeppson? This is Captain Ortiz."

Terri sat up in the bed. "Yes, captain."

"Thank you for the message about Mr. Herrick. He's a very important man. If word had leaked to the press that he was missing, there would have been a great uproar."

Terri had figured as much.

"You've managed to find out more information than our own police department, and have saved us a lot of grief. Now let us get down to business. Have you talked with your ex-husband yet?"

"No. But as I told you earlier, Mr. Herrick indicated Richard wasn't at a hospital so I'm not as worried. This morning I'm going to go to his work. If I can't find him there maybe you could send an officer to accompany me to his apartment. I need a translator to talk to the woman staying there. I have a feeling she'll know exactly where he is."

"If that becomes necessary, I will drive you there myself, *señora.*"

"Thank you very much. I'll stay in touch."

Fortified with a big breakfast, Terri left the hotel for Mr. Herrick's office. The same receptionist was on duty in the lobby of the building. When Terri explained what she wanted, the other woman shook her head.

"It's a long way from here and difficult to locate unless you're familiar with the area. To save you the trouble, I'll make a phone call to find out if he reported for work this morning. If he is there, then I will give you directions. A moment, *por favor.*"

Terri nodded.

While she waited, she couldn't help but wonder if Mr. Herrick had already been bombarded with visitors this morning. At least when they showed up, they would find the same man they knew. *Instead of a mummy facsimile.*

Terri had tried to imagine what he looked like under all those bandages. But maybe it was better she didn't know. Better that he remain her phantom friend. The man without a face.

Except for a pair of gorgeous gray eyes.

They were the portals to the inner man with whom she felt connected in an inexplicable way. Yet if she admitted as much to her sister, Beth would tell her she was being ridiculous.

Maybe she was.

"Señora Jeppson?"

Terri turned to the receptionist whose frowning expression clearly meant more bad news.

"According to your husband's supervisor, he hasn't been to work for three days, and didn't report this morning. He thinks your husband probably quit on him because there's been some trouble with him lately."

That sounded like Richard and didn't surprise Terri a bit.

"Thank you for inquiring. Would you do me one more favor?"

She gave the receptionist Captain Ortiz's number and asked her to get him on the phone. Within a few minutes he came on the line and made arrangements to pick her up in front of the office. He would drive her out to Richard's apartment.

An hour later the captain pulled his police car to the side of the street in front of the building Terri had visited yesterday.

He turned to her. "You remain here. I will go to the door first. If I think it is necessary, I'll come back out and signal for you to follow."

"All right."

Fifteen minutes passed before she saw him walk toward her. When he got back behind the wheel, he turned in her direction.

"Your ex-husband wasn't there. The woman in question is named Juanita Rosario. She says she has been living with him for ten months, which could or could not be the truth. According to her, they met soon after he found a job down here with the Herrick Company.

"It seems he left for work four days ago and never came home from his job. At first she wasn't worried. She said there are times when he parties with his friends and doesn't show up until the following day. But he's never been gone this long before.

''When you knocked on her door yesterday, she was afraid you were his wife. He'd told her he'd been trying to get a divorce from you, but you wouldn't let him.''

Terri shook her head. It sounded like the same old Richard. Lies, lies, lies to suit his particular purpose at the moment. No one hated commitment as much as Richard did.

''I told her you were his ex-wife from America, that you had divorced him a year ago. At that point she broke down. Now she is afraid he's gone off with some new woman for a while. But she's certain he'll be back because he's excited about their baby which is going to be born next month.''

''I hope she's right,'' Terri murmured. ''Unfortunately my ex-husband has a pattern of disappearing when he's really needed. How is the woman supporting herself?''

''He's been taking care of her.''

A groan escaped her throat. ''Does she have any family who will help look after her if he has deserted her?''

''No. She came from an abusive home and boyfriend.''

''Captain? We've got to find Richard. If nothing else, she needs him right now.''

The other man eyed her speculatively. ''At the moment it appears Mr. Herrick appears to know more about your ex-husband than anyone else.''

Her eyes closed tightly. ''I'm afraid you're right. If you'll drop me off at the hospital, I'll try to find out what else he knows.''

''While you do that, I'll send some officers to the work site to make inquiries. Maybe one of his co-workers knows something of importance and isn't aware of it.''

''Before we go, I'd like to see Juanita for a minute.'' She rummaged in her purse for her wallet. ''I'll be right back.''

He looked like he was about to say something, then thought the better of it.

She jumped out of the police car and hurried into the apartment building, tiptoeing past the same children who'd been playing on the stairs yesterday. The only cash she had on her was a hundred dollars, but it might help the pregnant woman get along for a few more days.

This time when she knocked, the door opened a little wider because there was no chain guard.

"Juanita?"

"*Si?*" She sounded hurt as well as angry this time.

"*Captain Ortiz dice que Richard no esta aqui ahora.*" Undoubtedly Terri was making every language error possible, but she had to try to communicate.

The other woman glared at her.

"*Tengo dinero para usted.*" Terri held out several bills.

Juanita didn't make a move to take them.

"*Por favor.*"

"*Por que?*" she bit out.

Why? Because I know exactly how you feel to be abandoned at the last moment.

Maybe if Terri said it was for the baby. "*Es necessario para el nino, verdad?*"

Juanita's face closed up. She had her pride. This had probably been the wrong thing to do, but if Richard didn't come back...

Unable to say the rest in Spanish she murmured, "In case you change your mind, I'll leave the money here."

She put the bills on the ground and hurried away without looking back.

The engine was idling when Terri returned to the car. Within seconds they were off.

Captain Ortiz drove a few miles before he said, "You are a kind person, but I'm afraid it was a mistake to give her money."

"If I were in her shoes, I would hope someone would do it for me. It will buy her food for a few more days. Perhaps by then we'll have found Richard."

"Let us hold that thought," he muttered, but he didn't sound as if he believed it any more than she did.

CHAPTER THREE

As TERRI entered Mr. Herrick's hospital room, she could smell flowers. Obviously the word had gone out he was here because a dozen fabulous arrangements had been brought in on carts. A huge fruit basket stood near his closet door.

Which gift was from his wife? Had Martha Shaw sent one, too?

Stop it, Terri. It's nothing to do with you.

She looked around. His room held wall-to-wall chairs. Someone had been to visit already. The clothes she'd bought him were no longer visible. As for the man in question, neither he nor the IV stand were anywhere in sight.

The door to the bathroom had been left ajar. He wasn't in there. Anxious to know if he was all right, she rushed out of the room and down the hall to the nursing station.

But before she reached it, an animated group of people turned the corner in her direction. She would have walked right past them if she hadn't caught sight of the dark-haired man in the center who was dressed in a navy robe and pajamas.

As Terri's gaze flew to his, she felt the impact of his piercing eyes and her feet came to a complete standstill.

It didn't matter that he had dressings at his hairline and beneath his strong chin. The ruggedly handsome face that went with those unforgettable gray eyes took her breath. No preconceived notion of the features she'd imagined hidden beneath the mask could live up to the vital, living presence of Benjamin Herrick.

When she realized the group's conversation had stopped

and everyone was staring at her because Mr. Herrick had refused to move on, her cheeks went hot. She knew she had to say something.

"I-I'm afraid we're all at a disadvantage. I'm Terri Jeppson."

"You're the woman Martha told us about," the older man in the Stetson interjected in a Texas accent. "If it hadn't been for you discovering the mix-up, our family wouldn't have known Ben was even in here. We're indebted to you, Mrs. Jeppson.

"I'm Ben's father, Dean." He shook hands with her. "This is my wife, Blanche, our daughter Leah and our son Parker. Our other son Creighton and his wife are on vacation and Leah's husband Grant couldn't make it, otherwise they would have flown down with us."

Everyone said hello.

Terri muttered an appropriate greeting, but relief that Leah wasn't Ben Herrick's wife dominated her chaotic emotions. Of course it didn't mean he wasn't married. Or engaged. Or living with a woman...

"I'm pleased to meet you," Parker said with a dashing smile. He let go of the IV stand to shake Terri's hand. His charm reminded her a little of Richard who knew he was attractive to women.

Like his father, he wore a Stetson. She thought he looked younger than his brother Ben who appeared to be in his mid-thirties. Both men bore a strong facial resemblance to their lovely mother, whereas sandy-haired Leah took after their father.

"Is your husband all right?" Mrs. Herrick asked in a compassionate tone of voice.

My ex-husband.

"I think so, but I haven't caught up with him yet."

Terri didn't want to believe Richard would shirk his

responsibility for his pregnant girlfriend at this late date. Hopefully he'd show up before too much longer.

Refusing to look at the silent man for fear he'd read too much feeling in her eyes, Terri said, "It's been very nice meeting all of you, but at this point I'm sure Mr. Herrick is tired after his walk. He probably wants to lie down. Now that I know he's with his family, I'll go."

"Don't worry about Ben. He's tough." His father patted his son's left shoulder. "But since the doctor said this is his first day out of bed, you may have a point."

As Terri started to walk toward the elevator around the corner, she heard a distinct groan of protest. It was a familiar sound. Loud enough to wake the dead, but she kept on going.

Already emotionally involved in ways she wasn't ready to examine, she knew any more time spent in his company could only backfire on her. The best thing to do was head for the hotel and stay put until she heard from Captain Ortiz.

"Mrs. Jeppson? Wait up!"

Terri had just emerged from the elevator on the main floor when Parker Herrick approached. He put a detaining hand on her arm. Then he grinned.

"You move faster than a nervous filly trying to outrun a twister." The analogy made her chuckle. "If there hadn't been another elevator going down, I would have missed you. My brother wants you to come back upstairs."

"I'll visit him again before I fly home to the States."

He shook his head. "Not good enough. He's more upset than I've ever seen him. If you don't show, there'll be hell to pay."

"Tell him I'll come by later when he doesn't have family around. I don't want to impose."

Parker pushed his hat back on his head. "We've been here six hours and that's longer than we've all been corralled together at one time in I don't know how many years.''

In spite of her misgivings, she laughed.

His gray-blue eyes twinkled. ''Knowing my brother, he was ready to throw us out ten minutes after we got here. It'll be doing the whole family a real favor if you'd be willing to baby-sit for a while.

''You see,'' he said in a confiding voice, ''the hospital staff's been singing your praises. With you here, Mom will feel like we can leave for an hour to grab a bite to eat.''

After having to fly down here at a moment's notice, Terri could well imagine how tired and hungry they were. It would be churlish to refuse when she'd come here with every intention of trying to get more information out of Mr. Herrick about Richard.

''All right. I'll go back with you, but I can't stay long.''

''That's fine. Anything to appease big brother.''

They turned and entered the next elevator going up.

''When will his wife be joining him?'' She had to know.

He slanted her an enigmatic glance. ''That's the question the folks have been asking since the day he left home to do his own thing years ago.''

Left home?

''You mean he and his wife are separated?''

''I mean, there *is* no Mrs. I figure that's the reason he's so testy, but don't let him know I told you that.''

Terri's heart started to thud. ''Why not?'' she teased.

''Because it's a taboo subject with him, and he told me I was a fool to get married. Now that I'm divorced, it's a case of I told you so. But as far I'm concerned, that doesn't mean marriage isn't the greatest while it's good.''

Terri didn't know. Hers had never really gotten off the ground. ''Do you have children, Parker?''

''No, thank the Lord.''

''I'm glad your divorce hasn't scarred you.''

"I refuse to let it. Next time I'll just make certain I marry the right woman."

"Are your other brother and sister happily married?"

"I think so. How about you and your husband?"

Thankfully they'd reached the sixth floor. With people getting in and out of the elevator, she was saved from having to answer his question. At this point it was better to remain closed mouth about Richard.

Terri reached the room ahead of Parker. Ben was sitting on the edge of the hospital bed surrounded by his family. The second Mrs. Herrick saw Terri she looked relieved and stood up.

"I'm so glad Parker found you in time, Mrs. Jeppson. We're sorry if our presence chased you away. Ben acted so upset when you left, I sent Parker after you. Please stay and talk to him as you had intended to do.

"Darling—" She turned to her unsmiling son whose somber gaze was leveled on Terri. "We're going to the Ramada, but we'll be back later to spend the rest of the time with you." She kissed his cheek.

Everyone said goodbye and filed out of the room except Parker. He stared at Terri.

"Are you by any chance staying at the Ramada, too?"

"No. The Ecuador Inn."

"I asked because we'll be eating an early dinner at the hotel and would have asked you to join us. If you're going to be here when we get back, we could bring you something to eat."

"That's very thoughtful of you, Parker, but I have other plans. Thank you anyway."

He tipped his hat. "Maybe we'll see you tomorrow then. Catch up with you later, Ben."

His brother nodded.

The minute Parker went out the door, Terri put her purse

on the side table, then turned to the man whose mere presence had such a profound effect on her senses.

"You've got a wonderful family, but it's good they left. You look exhausted." Without conscious thought, she knelt down and pulled the sandals off his feet. "Come on. Let's get your legs up on the bed."

As she helped lift them onto the mattress, he lay back against the pillow with a deep sigh.

She quickly covered him with the sheet. "There. I'm sure that feels much better."

While she adjusted the position of the IV stand holding his drip, he reached out with his left hand and clasped her forearm. Now that he only had a gauze dressing taped to his palm, he could flex his fingers whose tops were just as bronzed as the rest of him.

Her gaze darted to his. There was that look of pain and urgency in his eyes again.

"You obviously have something you're determined to tell me. Is it about Richard?"

He nodded.

"I'm glad. It's the reason why I came back to the hospital. No one has seen him in four days—not his immediate boss—not even the pregnant woman he's been living with. She's almost ready to deliver and needs him desperately."

Ben let go of her arm to point at the side table. Other than flowers, all she could see was her purse.

"Oh—I think I know what you have in mind."

As she reached for it, he nodded more emphatically.

Terri opened it to pull out a pen and the envelope that held her airline tickets.

"Here. You can write on the back of this. But please don't do it if it will hurt your hand. We could play the alphabet game again."

The noise he made sounded like a definite no.

She put the pen in his hand before placing the envelope near his knee where he'd bent his leg. She held on to it while he printed a short message with seemingly little difficulty.

When he'd finished, she took the pen and envelope from him, then read it. *"He was knocked unconscious by the boat. Died at sea with two others. Wanted to tell you first night. Forgive me."*

"Oh, no," she gasped. "Richard..."

As the tears sprang to her eyes, she felt Ben's hand on her arm once more. When she ventured another look into those gray depths, she understood why they'd been filled with pain, why they were alive with it now.

"You saw them drown?" she whispered, wiping the moisture from her cheeks.

He nodded solemnly.

"How ghastly." Her voice shook. "For *all* of you." After her quiet sobs subsided she said, "To think Richard died without even seeing his child born. Juanita will be inconsolable."

With startling speed he reached for the pen in her hand. When she realized his intentions, she placed the envelope on his leg once more.

He printed another message.

"Baby probably not his."

"That's what Captain Ortiz said. Juanita told him she'd been living with Richard for ten months."

"Came to work for company four months ago."

She pursed her lips. "Do you think it's possible they got together someplace else first?"

Terri felt his hesitation before he wrote, *"Prior job in Baton Rouge."*

"I doubt Juanita was ever in Louisiana. Dear God. When she hears the news that he died, it might bring on a miscarriage. At eight months, that would be so unbearably painful. I—I suffered two miscarriages, but at least they happened in the first trimester.''

Suddenly she felt his hand reach out to cover hers. He squeezed it gently and would pay a painful price, but the gesture sent a healing warmth through her body. She lifted her eyes. His brimmed with concern and compassion.

Terri was swept away by emotions so intense, she was afraid of them. Removing her hand she said, "D-do you have a rule about employees having to be married to work for you?''

He shook his head.

"I can't figure out why Richard said he was still married to me on his job application.''

Once more he took the pen from her other hand and put the envelope against his leg. He wrote, *"Wishful thinking."*

"No,'' she declared in a firm voice.

After eyeing her for an overly long moment he put, *"Have idea. Wait till I can talk."*

Guilt assailed her. For a moment she'd forgotten how absolutely miserable he was. His hand was probably killing him.

"Forgive me, Mr. Herrick. I'm sure all this writing couldn't have been good for your burned palm. In fact I'm afraid I've worn you out with my questions. While you rest, I'm going back to the hotel. I have phone calls to make to Captain Ortiz and my family.''

She put the pen and envelope in her purse.

"Is there anything I can do for you before I go?''

He tried to talk. It sounded like "come back.'' His throat had to be a lot better, *thank heaven.*

"I'll drop by tomorrow. On my way out, I'll ask one of the sisters to look in on you. Now that you've unburdened yourself, there's nothing more for you to worry about except getting well. Please try to sleep. Your family will be back here before you know it.''

As she turned to go, his phone rang.

''I'll get it,'' she volunteered.

Hurrying around the other side of the bed, she lifted the receiver. ''Hello?''

''Leah?'' a female voice questioned.

''No. This is Terri Jeppson.''

''Terri—'' The other woman sounded shocked. ''It's Martha Shaw.''

''Hello, Ms. Shaw. You barely missed Mr. Herrick's family. They're staying at the Ramada.''

''I know. I made the arrangements for them. What I didn't realize was that *you* were still there.''

Uh-oh. ''I was just on my way back to the hotel. Would you like to talk to Mr. Herrick?''

''Please.'' She was upset.

''Just a minute. He still can't answer yet.''

''I'm aware of that.'' Her chilly attitude reminded Terri of Juanita's.

''Here he is.''

When she went to put the phone to his ear, he pushed it away with his left hand. Terri wished she'd never bothered to answer it in the first place.

''Ms. Shaw? I-I'm afraid Mr. Herrick is in too much pain to deal with a phone call right now.''

There was a click. The line had gone dead.

She hung up the phone. ''Ms. Shaw was obviously disappointed. I would imagine she'll try again tomorrow. Now I have to go.''

This was one time Ben didn't feel he had the right to call her back. He knew for himself she was no longer in love with her ex-husband. But he was also aware that once upon a time she'd loved him enough to marry him.

Certain memories would never go away. Right now she

needed some time to herself to deal with the fact that he had died.

But when she left the room, it was as if she'd taken all the light with her. He felt empty and dissatisfied. Terri Jeppson was to blame for his emotional state. She was without a doubt the most remarkable, unique woman he'd ever met. He found himself craving her company more and more. When she'd told him about her miscarriages, he'd wanted to hold her in his arms and take the pain away.

Terri hurried down the hall and found Sister Angelica. After asking her to look in on their patient, she left the hospital.

When she finally reached her hotel room, the first thing she did was phone Captain Ortiz. To her chagrin he'd turned on his voice mail. She gave him what information she had, then she called her mother.

"Terri, honey? I'm so glad to hear from you. Did you find Richard?"

"Oh, Mom—" After breaking down, she told her mother everything she knew to this point in time. Except for the part about Juanita.

"I'm going to fly down there, honey. You shouldn't have to be alone to deal with everything."

"Much as I appreciate the thought, Mom, you can't come. You don't have a passport."

"That's right—I forgot."

"Which is entirely understandable," Terri murmured. "The only reason I was allowed to enter the country was because they thought I was married to Richard, therefore they granted me that special family emergency visa."

"How can I help you, honey?"

"Whether they find his body or not, I'll fly home tomorrow. Once I get there, we can put our heads together about whether we should hold a memorial service for him in Spearfish or Lead."

"I'm glad you're coming home, but what I meant was, what can I do to ease your heartache?"

"I did my grieving a long time ago, Mom. What I'm feeling now is sadness that his life was cut short. I don't think Richard ever found happiness." But maybe Terri was wrong. Maybe Juanita had been able to accomplish what no other woman had. Oh, poor Juanita.

"Well, we know he's happy where he is now, don't we."

"Yes. That brings me the greatest comfort." She sniffed. "Will you tell Beth? Right now I've got something I have to do. I'll call you back in the morning and let you know when my flight will be in."

"We'll be waiting to hear from you. God bless you, honey."

After Terri hung up, she glanced at her watch. Ten after three. If she left for Richard's apartment now, she could beat the late-afternoon traffic.

Grabbing some bottled water from the guest bar, she put it in her purse. As she reached for the extra roll she'd saved from breakfast, her phone rang.

She hurriedly picked up the receiver and said hello, expecting to hear Captain Ortiz on the other end.

"Mrs. Jeppson? This is Parker Herrick."

Her heart plummeted to her feet. "Has your brother suffered a relapse or something?"

"Not that I'm aware of," he drawled. "My folks wanted to know if you'd join us for dinner. Mom found out from the staff that you were the one who bought Ben his new night clothes. It's her way of saying thank you."

Relieved Ben was all right she said, "That's very nice of her, but I'm afraid I can't. I have an errand to run that could take me the rest of the afternoon and evening."

"Would you like some company?"

Why was he pressing? Unless... Did Martha feel so

threatened, even by a married woman, that she would ask Parker to keep tabs on Terri?

"You don't happen to speak Spanish, do you?"

"Our whole family does. We have to."

If he went with her, she'd have to confide some things to him. But that was all right. He'd been through a divorce too and would understand. If he could allay Martha's fears and translate for Terri at the same time, then it would be worth it. Hopefully Juanita would still be at the apartment.

"If you really don't mind, I admit I could use your help."

"Good. When shall I pick you up?"

"As soon as possible."

"I'm on my way. I'll be driving a white Land Rover with the words Herrick Corporation on the side."

"I'll be waiting out front."

As soon as Terri hung up, she unwrapped the roll and ate it to give herself a little sustenance. Once she'd rinsed her face and run a brush through her hair, she put on a fresh coat of lipstick.

Feeling more presentable, she left the room and hurried downstairs to the bank. She'd brought a thousand dollars with her. If she cashed five hundred dollars worth of travelers' checks, she'd still have enough money to get home.

It didn't matter what Captain Ortiz said. Juanita Rosario needed help, and Richard was no longer alive to give it. If there wasn't a baby on the way that would be different, but the woman was practically ready to deliver. Maybe it was ridiculous, but Terri felt responsible for her welfare even if Richard wasn't the father.

Terri only hoped Juanita's pride wouldn't prevent her from taking it. Parker might have to do some fast talking.

Poor Parker. He didn't have the faintest idea what he was getting into. But forty-five minutes later, after directing him to the outskirts of the city while they drove in air-conditioned luxury, she'd explained the situation to him.

When he pulled up in front of the apartment, he cocked his head to look at her.

"You know what I think?"

"I already know."

"I don't think you do. I was just going to say how much I admire you, a divorced woman, coming to the aid of a fellow human being, especially under these circumstances."

Parker didn't know about Terri's miscarriages. That was personal. But the fact was, her whole family had been there for her when she'd gone through them. Who would help Juanita?

"That's my job back home," she quipped, fighting the tears that were threatening. "Thanks, Parker. I needed to hear those words because I'm determined about this. I doubt Juanita has very many resources, if any."

"We'll find out. Shall we go in?"

Terri nodded and climbed down from the seat. He left his cowboy hat in the car before they walked the short distance to Richard's apartment. She knocked on the door.

This time when Juanita peered through the opening of the chain, Terri could see she was dressed in a sleeveless pale blue shift. The woman's face had streak marks, as if she'd been crying.

Stifling a groan, Terri looked to Parker for help.

She'd chosen the right person. After introducing himself in fluent Spanish, he began to explain what had happened. Terri could follow some of it. She knew the moment Juanita heard the truth about Richard.

The other woman burst into a paroxysm of tears that was heart wrenching to witness. Parker waited, then said something else. Eventually Juanita quieted down enough to lift her head and look at Terri.

"What did you say to her?"

"That you were grieving, too, because he'd once been your husband."

Parker didn't know everything going on in Terri's mind, but it didn't matter. He'd said the right thing to Juanita. Terri could only admire him for that.

"Will you tell her the only reason I'm here is to make sure she'll be able to have her baby without worrying about money? Tell her I'm sorry I don't have more to give."

While Parker explained everything, Terri handed Juanita the five hundred dollars. The other woman's hand trembled as she took it.

In a surprise move, Parker pulled out his billfold and added his own generous donation. "Please accept this from the Herrick Corporation," he said in Spanish.

Juanita appeared to hesitate before her fingers closed over the bills he pressed in her other hand.

"*Gracias, señor,*" she murmured in a wobbly voice. Her liquid-brown eyes swerved to Terri. "*Muchas gracias, señora.*"

"Parker?" Terri whispered. "Tell her that if she needs anything else, she can reach me through Captain Ortiz at the main police station. I'll write his number down for her." She tore off a piece of paper from her purse and copied it for her.

"Oh—and tell her something else. Let her know I'll be praying for her and her baby."

Parker seemed to have trouble swallowing before he addressed the other woman and gave her the paper.

"*Gracias,*" she heard Juanita whisper before she shut the door on them.

"The poor thing." Terri wept all the way to the car.

Once they were inside he said, "Do you always get this emotionally involved with strangers?"

She sniffed. "No. Of course not."

He started the engine and they pulled away from the building. "Then how do you account for the clothes you bought for Ben? For that matter, why did my brother fall apart when you left him earlier today? He didn't behave like the man I've always known."

"Probably because he almost lost his life in the accident that took my ex-husband's, and he's feeling vulnerable."

"Vulnerable is not a word one associates with Ben. Even Martha remarked to Creighton how surprised she was that you had taken such a personal interest in him."

"That's because she's in love with Ben." The comment slipped out before Terri realized she'd verbalized her thoughts.

"How did you pick up on that so fast?" he asked in a quiet tone.

"Instinct."

More than anything Terri wanted to ask if Ben Herrick was in love with his brother's secretary. But she didn't dare, and Parker didn't seem inclined to satisfy her curiosity.

They rode the rest of the way into the city without talking. She finally turned to him. "I can't thank you enough for what you did for me this afternoon. One day you'll know my gratitude."

"If you mean that, have dinner with me."

She hoped it was an oversight and he'd meant to say "with the family."

"Thank you, but I can't. Captain Ortiz could be calling me right now. I'm waiting to find out if Richard's body has been recovered from the accident scene."

Parker drew up in front of the hotel and stopped the car. "If you need me for anything, call the hospital. I'll be there with Ben."

"I'm sure he's grateful to have his family around at a

time like this.'' She climbed out. ''Thanks again more than I can say for the ride and your translating services.''

''I wanted to help. I'd like to do a lot more if you'd let me.''

There was no mistaking what he'd implied just now. He reminded her a little of the man she'd had dinner with in Lead on the night she'd received the call from Martha Shaw. Both men had been hurt by their divorces and were anxious to find someone else to love, but Terri wasn't that person.

She shut the door. Through the open window she said, ''You did that when you contributed to Juanita's welfare. It was a very kind thing to do.''

He eyed her briefly before putting his hat back on. ''I'll see *you* tomorrow.''

Terri shut the door without giving him a response.

Though she'd told Ben Herrick she'd drop by the hospital, she knew in her heart of hearts it wouldn't be a good idea. Everything was getting much too complicated.

Better to return to her life in South Dakota as soon as possible. Immersed in her work, she'd be too busy to think about how much she'd enjoyed her time with the bandaged stranger when he'd had no identity, no title, no family and no history that included Martha Shaw.

Twenty minutes later Terri had spoken with Captain Ortiz. He'd obtained the name and address of the fisherman, but so far the police hadn't been able to talk to him. As for bodies, none had turned up in the vicinity the fisherman had described to the hospital authorities. However they did find some pieces of debris which might belong to the boat in question.

As for the other two drowning victims mentioned by Mr. Herrick, they weren't employees of his company. The only person who'd been reported missing from work was Richard. That news made the case more complicated.

Depending on the actual site of the accident and the ocean current, it might be days or weeks before any bodies were recovered. If ever.

According to the captain, he intended to visit Mr. Herrick that evening. If it didn't hurt the burn on his hand too much, he would ask him to write down a few facts about the accident on paper. His testimony would make all the difference.

Terri agreed. Before she hung up, she told him there was nothing more to keep her in Guayaquil. She planned to fly back to South Dakota in the morning. If anything came up, the captain had her phone number and address in Lead.

He bid her a safe journey home. When they'd rung off, she phoned for room service, then called the airline and made a reservation for the flight leaving for Atlanta at nine forty-five in the morning.

After her dinner arrived, she lay on the bed and ate while she discussed everything with Beth.

"You've taken Richard's death a lot better than I thought you would."

"I think it's because I know he had someone who loved him right up to the end. Juanita's very young. You could tell she idolized him. He would have liked that."

"You're right."

Terri finished the last of her crab salad. "Juanita's the one I feel sorry for."

"You did all you could. Honestly, Terri, I don't know that many ex-wives who would throw their hard-earned money at their former husband's lover!"

"She's going to have a baby."

"It's not even his!"

"I know, but she was depending on Richard."

"I still say your heart is made of mush. So tell me about the head of the Herrick Corporation. What's he like?"

Terri's heart raced. "I-it's hard to say. He's still hooked up to an IV and has dressings taped to his stitches. The doctors won't let him talk yet."

"Then how did you find out about Richard?"

Heat filled her cheeks. "It's a long story." Terri didn't dare tell her sister how she'd played a variation of the same game with him she'd played with Beth when they were children. "We managed to communicate. He finally wrote down a few words."

"I thought his hands were burned."

"Just the palms."

"It's so bizarre to think it wasn't Richard lying there."

"You can't imagine." Terri's voice trembled.

"What tipped you off? Mom never said."

Mom doesn't know.

"When they took the oxygen mask away, I saw his eyes. T-they were gray instead of blue," she stammered. "Listen, Beth, I'd better hang up. This call is costing me a fortune. I'll see you and Mom tomorrow."

"Can't wait till you're home. I want to hear all the details. We'll be waiting for you at the airport in Rapid City. Have a safe flight."

After their phone call, Terri showered and packed before crawling into bed. Unfortunately she was wide-awake and restless, haunted by the events of the last few days.

Angry at herself for reliving certain moments she needed to forget for her own good, she turned on the television to provide some background noise. There was a tourist magazine on the table that told where to eat and what to see in Guayaquil. She took it to bed with her and read until oblivion took over.

CHAPTER FOUR

BEN gave his family time to reach the elevator before he sat up and pulled the IV needle carefully out of his arm.

After levering himself from the hospital bed, he removed his sling, then took off his pajamas. Once he'd dressed in the new clothes his parents had purchased, he put the sling back on. He stuffed the clothes and sandals Terri had bought for him in a plastic bag and started for the door.

Dr. Dominguez appeared in the hallway. "Where do you think you are going this early on a Monday morning?"

"My throat feels much better," Ben whispered. "I have work to do."

The doctor stood there for a moment before nodding his head. "All right, but you shouldn't be alone at home."

"I have someone in mind who will take care of me."

"That's good. Come to the nursing station. Sister Angelica will give you some information for the care of your cuts as well as a soft food regimen. Make an appointment to return in a week. I need to see how your stitches are healing. Be careful when you shave."

"I will. Thank you, Doctor. I'm indebted to all of you on the staff here for your excellent care. Please feel free to distribute the flowers and fruit basket to any patients who will enjoy them."

"They'll be much appreciated, Mr. Herrick. Thank *you.*"

A few minutes later Ben emerged from the front doors of the hospital to hail Carlos Rivera, his manager and right hand at the work site.

The night before, Ben had asked Sister Angelica to phone Carlos and notify him that he was at San Lorenzo Hospital. It hadn't taken Carlos long to show up.

Using pen and paper, Ben had told the other man to pick him up early the next morning. Carlos could always be counted on to follow through without asking a lot of irritating questions.

"You have no idea how good it feels to get out of there!"

"I can imagine. Where to now?"

"The Ecuador Inn. Step on it!"

When Terri's alarm went off at quarter to seven, she didn't feel at all rested. Upset with herself because her thoughts had been on Ben Herrick rather than Richard, she realized she ought to be thankful she was leaving the country.

Knowing she needed food before a long flight, she ordered breakfast. Years ago she'd learned that she could skip other meals, but breakfast she couldn't do without.

While she waited for it to come, she dressed for the trip in a short-sleeved blue cotton sweater with matching pants and bone-colored leather sandals.

Her haircut made it easy to brush into place. The sun had streaked it here and there, making her look more blond than she really was. With the moderate tan she'd acquired over the summer, she could wear coral lipstick. A touch of Fleurs de Rocaille on her throat and wrists, and she was ready.

Worried because she needed to be at the airport two hours before her flight was called, she let out a sigh of relief when she heard the knock on the door.

"*Buenos di—*" Terri started to say to the waiter after opening it, then let out a gasp, almost fainting from shock.

Someone tall and dark she'd never expected to see again

in her life stood there dressed in a cream-colored sport shirt and trousers. He wore his arm in a sling.

Her anxious blue gaze flew to his. "What on earth are you doing out of the hospital?" she cried angrily, fearing for his safety. "Are you insane?"

"Most people think so," Ben Herrick whispered with maddening calm.

She couldn't help but stare at his striking male features. "You're not supposed to be talking yet!"

His lips twitched. "I thought you'd be happy I could make any sounds at all."

"I am!" Terrie blurted. Her violent outburst seemed to fill the hallway. "Of course I am," she said in a quieter voice, trying to calm down. "I just didn't expect—"

"To see me again?" he broke in before she could finish.

By now her cheeks were on fire.

Just as Dr. Fortuna had said, Ben Herrick looked amazingly fit, especially for a person who'd just left his hospital bed after an ordeal that could have taken his life. The tape that held the IV needle still adhered to his bronzed skin above his left wrist.

"I—I was on my way to the airport."

His gray eyes narrowed on her upturned features. "Yes, I know. Captain Ortiz told me you planned to return to the States this morning. You weren't even going to come by my room to say goodbye."

Filled with guilt *and* dazed because he'd actually left the hospital and could talk—even if it was a forced whisper—she scarcely noticed the waiter who approached carrying her breakfast tray. She'd forgotten all about it.

"Buenos dias, señorita."

Terri murmured something appropriate and took the tray from him. "Just a minute while I find my purse."

"I'll take care of it." Mr. Herrick reached in his pocket with his free hand to pay the man a generous tip.

When the waiter had disappeared he said, "Aren't you going to invite me in?"

"Of course!" she snapped, feeling out of control. "You should be sitting down, you know." She moved out of the way so he could enter.

He shut the door behind him and walked over to the table, but he remained standing. After lifting the cover off the plate he said, "Your breakfast smells good. Go ahead and eat while it's hot."

In the excitement of seeing him again, she'd lost her appetite. "Why are you here, Mr. Herrick?"

His head turned in her direction. "The name is Ben. After what we've both been through together, I can't imagine your calling me anything else."

Her pulse raced. "If the doctor released you, then you should have gone straight home!"

"That's where I'm headed." He put the cover back. "I only stopped by the hotel long enough to take you with me."

She stood there in shock, convinced she hadn't understood him correctly.

"It's very simple," he continued to whisper, taking advantage of her silence. "Dr. Dominguez said I could leave as long as I had someone to watch out for me over the next few days."

Her legs started to tremble.

"You have a family anxious to do that for you."

"They're on their way back to Texas this morning."

"Why?"

"Because I asked them to leave."

Aghast she cried, "How could you do that when they flew all this way to be with you?"

"They *were* with me. The entire night. We had a very nice reunion. But I'm not up to entertaining them. At six this morning, I bid them goodbye.

"Now that I'm out of the hospital, I'd like to recuperate in my own home with someone who knows instinctively how to take care of my needs. If you'd be willing to postpone your travel plans for a few days, I'll make it worth your while."

"You mean you want me to act as your nurse." Memories of the massage she'd given his legs refused to go away.

"I simply want you to be yourself," he said, shifting his weight.

Terri darted him an anxious glance, afraid he was feeling weak after his ordeal.

One dark brow dipped lower than the other. "Did I misunderstand you when you told me your work at the chamber of commerce consisted of doing a little bit of everything?"

"No—" She hadn't meant to sound cross, not when anger was the last emotion she was experiencing. Excitement would be more like it. A growing excitement she couldn't seem to contain.

"Then that's all I'm asking," he said reasonably. "According to the doctor, I'm supposed to be on a liquid diet today. Depending on how my throat feels tomorrow, I may be able to tolerate some soft food.

"If you could take care of the meals and answer my phone for me, do a little correspondence while this arm is in a sling, I'd be grateful."

Her eyes traveled to his palms which the dressings still covered. She'd worried he'd done more injury to his hand when he'd written those messages at the hospital. Of course he would never complain about the pain. As she'd already discovered, Ben Herrick was no ordinary man.

It was on the tip of her tongue to ask why he hadn't sent for Martha Shaw. She had an idea his brother's secretary would sell her soul to be in Terri's shoes right now.

But he probably had his male pride and didn't want the other woman to see him like this. At least not until he'd recovered and no longer needed to wear dressings over his stitches. Since Terri had already been around him during his worst moments, no doubt he felt comfortable in her presence.

"There's another reason I want you stay," he added.

Alert to a different inflection in his voice, her breath caught.

"Captain Ortiz came to the hospital last night. With the information I gave him, your ex-husband's body could possibly be found in the next few days. Since you would have to identify it before it could be shipped back to South Dakota for burial, remaining in Guayaquil will save you another trip to Ecuador."

Now that she knew the real reason for his extraordinary request, she suffered a vicious stab of disappointment. In fact it almost incapacitated her. She averted her eyes.

There was no mystery here.

The man was only trying to spare her the grief of an unnecessary flight later on. Manufacturing a job as his nursemaid would give her something constructive to do while she waited for word from the police.

Before she could give him an answer, there was another rap on the door. His inquiring gray gaze met hers. "Are you expecting someone?"

"Earlier I told the desk I was checking out. They've probably sent a bellboy to help with my luggage. Excuse me."

She hurried past him and opened the door.

"Parker—" she blurted in complete surprise.

"Good morning."

Terri quickly stifled a groan. "What are you doing here?"

"Isn't it obvious?" He smiled before removing his cowboy hat.

"I thought you were on your way back to Texas."

"Plans have a way of changing. I'm glad I caught you in time. If you'd allow me, I'd like to drive you to the airport."

She felt Ben's presence behind her.

"I'm afraid Terri's not leaving the country for a while," came Ben's whisper.

As he drew alongside her she noticed he'd helped himself to her apple juice. After being fed intravenously, she imagined it tasted good sliding down his sore throat.

Ben's appearance wiped the charming smile from Parker's face. "Who let *you* out of the hospital?"

"I was just released with the proviso that Terri would be there to take care of me. But it was nice of you to offer her your services. We're both in your debt. Fortunately there's still time for you to make it to the airport and fly out with the rest of the family. That is, if you leave now," he added.

The less than subtle hint caused the younger man's eyes to glint with frustration and disappointment before they swerved to Terri's. "How long are you staying in Guayaquil?"

To her chagrin it didn't sound as if Parker was ready to give up. She supposed that trait was what made the Herrick men seem a little bigger than life. However in Parker's case, she should never have allowed him to drive her out to Richard's apartment. It had led him to believe she could be interested in him.

Though Terri hadn't yet agreed to Ben's proposition, he'd provided her with a perfect opportunity to send Parker the message that a relationship with him was out of the question.

"I really don't know yet."

She had the impression Ben drained the rest of his glass with satisfaction.

"Now that you've learned I'm in the best of hands, you can tell Mother to stop worrying about me."

"I probably won't leave until tomorrow," Parker said, stubbornly holding his ground. He eyed her directly. "As long as I'm here, how about dinner this evening?"

"If we didn't have other plans, we'd enjoy it," Ben responded before Terri could think up an excuse.

His speculative gaze flicked to Ben. "What other plans?"

"This is the soonest I could arrange for her to visit the site where her ex-husband died."

Terri blinked at the revelation, which had a sobering effect on Parker. He looked at her once more.

"I didn't realize." She could hear his mind working. "When you're back in South Dakota, I'll get in touch with you."

"It may not be for a while," Ben interjected. "She's still waiting for his body to be found. That *is* the reason why she came to Guayaquil in the first place."

Filling the uncomfortable silence she said, "I appreciate your offer to drive me to the airport, Parker. Thank you for all your help."

He twirled his hat before shoving it on his head. "You're welcome. Be expecting a call from me soon." It sounded like a vow. "Take it easy, Ben," he muttered before heading down the hall toward the elevators.

"Thanks for flying down with the family, Parker. It meant a lot to me." Ben closed the door, then leveled his penetrating gaze on her. "My brother has developed a crush on you. It happened fast."

"He's very nice."

"I agree."

"When he drove me to Richard's apartment, he told me he was divorced. I'm sure he's feeling lost."

"There's no doubt about it. But first he needs to find out who he is before he rushes headlong into another relationship."

It was good advice. The kind she'd disregarded by agreeing to be Ben's temporary nurse. Which reminded her that all this whispering couldn't be good for his throat.

She took the empty glass from him. "You should be home resting."

"You're reading my mind."

For all she knew, he was ready to collapse from weakness. "I assume you live in an apartment. Is it far from here?"

"It's a condo about forty-five miles away."

Forty-five? "That's a lot further than Richard's apartment."

"By about twenty miles," he concurred. "While you enjoy your breakfast, I'll tell Carlos to come up for your suitcase."

Was Ben friends with one of the bellboys?

Since she was the person who was supposed to be taking care of him, she decided she'd better follow his suggestion and eat so she wouldn't run out of energy.

The cold French toast and ham didn't taste half bad. After swallowing her milk, she rushed over to the phone and made a quick call to her mom, telling her about the change in plans. Promising to phone her later in the day with the details, she rang off and hurried into the bathroom to brush her teeth.

When she returned, she packed her cosmetic kit in the suitcase sitting on the bed.

"I'm ready," she announced to Ben who stood at the door with a deeply tanned Hispanic man. He wore a khaki shirt with the Herrick logo on the pocket. With a head of gleaming black hair and moustache, he was attractive in his own way.

"Mrs. Jeppson? This is Carlos Rivera, my office manager at the site. I couldn't function without him."

"How do you do, Mr. Rivera. I'm going to be his nurse for a while."

"It's a pleasure to meet you. Call me Carlos."

While he reached for her suitcase, she found her purse on the dresser. By tacit agreement the three of them left the room for the elevator.

"Carlos?" she said when they'd arrived at the foyer. "I have to check out. Since Mr. Herrick barely left his hospital bed, why don't you two wait for me in the car?"

"I was going to suggest it."

"Good. One more thing—he shouldn't be using his voice at all. If he does, gag him!"

Carlos laughed uninhibitedly before saying something to Ben in Spanish she couldn't follow.

Out of the corner of her eye she saw a smile curve Ben's compelling mouth. With her heart skidding in reaction to his devastating male appeal, she rushed across the tiles to the front desk to pay her bill. The receptionist said the Herrick company had already taken care of it.

Martha Shaw had already told her they would, but Terri felt she had to try. It didn't seem right they paid for everything.

Five minutes later she emerged from the hotel. Carlos stood next to the same kind of Land Rover that Parker had driven. As soon as he saw her, he opened the rear passenger door to help her inside.

After she'd thanked him and they'd merged with the morning traffic, she had an idea.

"Carlos? Mr. Herrick is on a special diet. When we come to a good supermarket, will you stop so I can buy the items he needs?"

"Of course."

She leaned forward and whispered in his ear. "Do you know if he has a video machine?" The other man nodded. "Then can you please drive us to a video shop, too. There are a couple of films I'd like to get."

"It's impolite to pretend I'm not here," Ben whispered.

"As far as I'm concerned, you're still the invisible man!"

As it had done the other day, his body shook with laughter.

"Mr. Herrick almost died in the accident and isn't supposed to be talking yet, Carlos. I suggest we ignore him."

"She's right, Ben. You let us take care of everything."

"Good grief. What have I done?" Even though he could only whisper, he'd said it in a mocking tone.

His question went unanswered as Terri sat back, picking out some of the landmarks that were becoming familiar to her on this third trip south. They'd driven about ten miles when Carlos stopped near a shopping center.

He looked over his shoulder. "I'll go in with you."

"Good."

Terri got out of the back seat. Ben's window had been lowered. "Is there anything else you want from the store besides food, Mr. Herrick? Don't speak. Just nod or shake your head."

Because she'd leaned closer, a delightful flowery fragrance assailed him, electrifying all his senses. Her blue cotton sweater revealed enticing curves and creamy skin. He could hardly concentrate on her question. One of these days he would get her to call him by his first name.

He finally had the presence of mind to shake his head.

"We'll be quick," she assured him before joining Carlos. They headed for the market in the center of a cluster of other stores.

His gaze narrowed on the mold of those long shapely

legs beneath her cotton pants. She had to be five-seven, five-eight. The perfect height for him.

By now every man in the parking area had caught sight of the attractive blond American. Her femininity stuck out a mile. How could he fault Parker for being entranced when so many male eyes followed Terri's progress into the market?

What in the hell could have possessed Richard Jeppson to roam when he had everything a man could desire waiting for him at home?

Fifteen minutes later the subject of his thoughts returned to the car with her arms full of groceries. She had Carlos in tow with a couple of bags. He looked surprisingly domestic. A half smile broke out on Ben's face. It would be a first for the man who was a confirmed bachelor.

"You're the only woman I've ever known who did her grocery shopping that fast," Ben couldn't help remarking. "Is that a midwestern trait?"

"As a matter of fact it *isn't*." Her eyes flashed blue sparks. "But since you should be home in bed with your mouth bound, I sped things up."

The two men chuckled while Terri helped Carlos put all the groceries in the back. After she'd shut herself inside, they were off.

"Okay, Carlos. Now that I'm a captive audience, tell me what Mr. Herrick does down in this part of the world. I thought most Texans were into cattle and oil."

"Ben doesn't exactly run true to form."

"So I've noticed."

"It might be easier to show you than try to explain. We'll be joining the coastal road any minute now. After we've been on it about twenty more miles, you'll see an amazing sight."

"You've aroused my curiosity. While I'm waiting with

bated breath, I think it's time for everyone to have a snack.''

She turned around and rummaged in the sacks until she found what she was looking for. ''Two cold colas for me and you, Carlos, and a can of delicious vegetable juice for you, Mr. Herrick. According to Carlos, it's just like the V-8 juice sold in the States.''

She popped the tab, then leaned forward to hand it to Ben. ''Before you complain that it isn't T-bone steak, just remember you were being fed through a tube an hour ago.''

''I'd like to forget,'' he whispered before drinking thirstily.

A powerfully built man like him would be ravenous for anything he could tolerate right now. It was a good thing she'd bought a large supply of food and drinks.

''When we get to your condo, I'll fix you some soup. For dessert, you can have ice cream. I bought chocolate, vanilla, mocha and orange sherbet.''

Pulling the tab on the cola, she handed a drink to Carlos. In the process, she noticed Ben had already drained his juice.

''I can see that just keeping you from the edge of starvation is going to be a *huge* project.'' After taking the empty can away she said, ''How about some peach nectar?''

''I think I'll hold out for the ice cream.''

''In case you hadn't noticed, I'm asking yes and no questions. All you have to do is nod or shake your head.''

Once again she could see his shoulders shake with laughter. Apparently it was contagious because Carlos burst into rich laughter, too. After the ordeal Ben had lived through, she was glad he seemed to be through the worst of his misery.

Having done all she could do for the moment, Terri sat back to drink her cola.

"Carlos? How long did it take you to realize Mr. Herrick was missing?"

The other man's dark eyes looked at her through the rearview mirror. "The last time Ben and I talked was on Monday. He told me he'd be in Miami until the end of the week finishing up some important business.

"I can always reach him on his cell phone. However nothing came up that needed his input, so I had no idea he'd been in an accident until a sister at the hospital phoned me last night."

Obviously Ben hadn't told Carlos where he was going before he planned to fly to Miami. Terri shuddered to realize he could have died and no one would have had any idea.

"It didn't happen, so don't think about it," Ben whispered. Even from the front seat where he couldn't see her, he had the ability to read her mind.

There was still a lot she didn't know about the circumstances leading up to Richard's death. Ben held all the answers. But until he could really speak without it hurting his throat, she would have to be patient.

"If you're through, Carlos, I'll take your can."

He handed it to her. She put it in the nearest sack with the others. As she sat back, another thought came to her.

"Do you have your cell phone? I'm afraid I forgot to cancel my flight."

"We took care of it while you were paying your bill," Carlos responded.

"Thank you. As for my bill, it had already been taken care of. Thank you, Mr. Herrick. That was very generous of you."

"We do it for family members if they have to come in an emergency."

After that remark, there was nothing to do but take in the scenery. Having come from a landlocked state in the U.S., being able to see the ocean in the distance as you drove along always provided a thrill.

The traffic was heavy even after they'd left the suburbs and residential areas behind. A loaded freight train ran parallel to their car, coming between them and the coast. A few more miles and the highway veered left, separating them from the train as they rose to a higher elevation.

At first she assumed they were headed inland. Then the car negotiated a curve, which took them south once more. That's when a vista opened up.

In the far distance Terri saw what looked like another huge city bordering an inlet of the ocean. In the middle was an island where a mammoth building rose at least twenty stories above the water. It had to be some kind of fabulous resort.

She grabbed the map the hotel had given her, positive this city wasn't on it. Sure enough when she searched the section south of Guayaquil, this place was nowhere to be found. How could that be?

Her head came up. "Did you know th—" But she never finished her sentence because she suddenly realized her mistake.

Closer now, she could see that this city was a giant shipyard. It was much bigger than the naval one she'd seen on the East Coast with her parents when she and Beth were a lot younger. Her gaze took in the building which wasn't quite as far away now.

"Good heavens—that's a *ship!* It's the most enormous thing I've ever seen in my life! I'm sure it's longer than a couple of aircraft carriers."

"Four to be exact," Carlos explained.

"You're kidding!" she cried. "I've been on one. They're about a thousand feet long."

"That's right. *The Spirit of Atlantis* is twenty-three stories tall from its main deck, 4100 feet long and 700 feet wide, almost three times the width of say, the *Kitty Hawk*."

She could hardly take it in. A ship close to a mile long...

"What is it? Ecuador's secret weapon?"

Both men laughed again.

"Seriously," she said. "Was it built for their military or something?"

"Not exactly," came Ben's whisper.

Carlos made a turn that took them closer to the water's edge. "You're looking at the floating city of the future. It was built by an American entrepreneur who along with other businessmen have brought prosperity to this country by offering employment to thousands of locals over the last few years.

"When the *Atlantis* sets sail on its maiden voyage next week, the shipyard will remain for the building and repair of other ships."

Terri shook her head.

A floating city...

The mind that had conceived anything this spectacular had to be some sort of genius. Naturally such a project would provide a boost to any country's economy.

"No wonder this captured my ex-husband's imagination. Were there many people hired from the States to work on it?"

"Several thousand. Many more thousands from the U.S. and other countries will be staffing it."

Her gaze switched to the maze of buildings, train tracks and giant cranes. As she scanned the busy scenes going on around her, she noticed one of the floating docks where she saw several oil tankers with the words Herrick emblazoned.

Terri sat forward. "My ex-husband was a glazier. How did he come to be hired by Mr. Herrick?"

She intercepted a private glance between Ben and Carlos before the latter said, "He *wasn't* hired by him."

"Then how come the Herrick Corporation called to tell me Richard was in the hospital?"

At this juncture they'd arrived at a pier. Carlos pulled to a stop, then turned around to look at her with a thoroughly puzzled expression.

"You really didn't know all this is Ben's brainchild?"

CHAPTER FIVE

"No," TERRI murmured. Yet she couldn't honestly say she was surprised. From the first moment she'd looked into the stranger's eyes, she'd felt there was something magnetic about him. Something that set him apart from other men.

Now she understood Captain Ortiz's words.

Mr. Herrick is a very important man. If the press had found out he was missing, it would have caused a great uproar.

"To be honest, Carlos, my ex-husband and I never communicated after our divorce. I had no idea he'd made the decision to work outside the U.S. The call from Houston came as a total surprise."

"As did the call I received from the hospital," Carlos remarked in a subdued tone.

Terri could well imagine the other man's shock. "After Mr. Herrick's horrifying ordeal, he ought to be resting. Where is his condo from here?"

"I live on the *Atlantis*. Shall we go?" Ben whispered hoarsely before climbing out of the car.

While Terri digested that amazing revelation, she rushed to gather up some of the grocery bags. Carlos took care of her suitcase and the other sacks.

Dozens of dock workers hailed Ben. While he chatted with those who'd gathered around, no doubt because of the sling he was wearing, another man rushed forward to assist Terri with the groceries. The whole time she felt Ben's unwavering gaze as she was helped into a tender,

78

one of dozens of boats that were used to ferry workers out to the huge ship.

In a moment he followed, refusing help from anyone. When he moved in her direction with that swift male agility she could only admire, her heart began pounding in outrageous fashion. In a few seconds he'd sat down on the banquette-type seat opposite her.

Carlos got in last with his load. After he'd placed everything on the floor, he handed out the life preservers. While Terri fastened hers, he helped Ben with his. Then he donned one himself and walked to the rear of the boat where a seaman revved the motor. He reversed at a wakeless speed to clear the other boats. Soon they were zooming away from the pier.

Terri had always adored the ocean, that unmistakable smell of salt in the air you could never get enough of. Today the water reflected a deep blue, causing the mammoth ship to stand out like bright white chalk on a new blackboard.

Through holes in the drifting clouds, the late-morning sun beat down on them. But there was a refreshing breeze which filmed their hot skin with a fine mist of sea spray.

Ben's black-brown hair curled at the tips, partially hiding the dressing at his hairline from view. The one under his chin was hardly noticeable. He looked disgustingly healthy for someone who'd had such a recent brush with death.

When he'd said he could use her help for a few days, she'd never dreamed it meant living on the water. The closer they drew to their destination, the more she marveled at such a massive feat of engineering.

"It's so fabulous, I'm speechless," she said when her eyes finally met his.

A smile hovered around his sensuous lips. The man's

arresting looks made it difficult to concentrate on anything else. She smothered a groan.

By the time they reached a center landing which led inside one of the ship's lower decks on the portside, Terri realized they had to be in very deep water. There wouldn't be that many natural harbors in the world that could handle anything this colossal.

She shuddered to think Richard had lost his life somewhere out here. Was it even possible to find him at these depths? Terri didn't honestly hold out any hope of his body being recovered.

In an unexpected move, Ben put a hand on her arm. "Don't think about it right now. I'll explain everything later when we're alone."

He always seemed to be on her wavelength. She nodded without looking at him. When he relinquished his hold, Carlos was standing by to gather their preservers and help her out of the tender into the ship. Several Hispanic stewards helped with the groceries and her suitcase.

She smiled at Carlos. "Aren't you coming with us?"

He shook his head. "I have work to do, but I'm sure we'll see each other again soon."

"Thank you for all your help."

"Amen to that," Ben added.

"It was my pleasure." He nodded to them both before getting back in the tender.

Once inside the ship, it felt like Terri had entered a hotel complete with rooms, stairways, corridors and elevators. Ben clasped her elbow and guided her along the hallway several hundred feet before unlocking the door to what was a small, private elevator.

"Just set the bags and suitcase on the floor," he instructed the stewards whose navy and white uniforms looked smart and professional.

After thanking them for their help, he pushed a button

and the door closed. Terri stood breathlessly close to the man who'd been haunting her dreams for the last few nights.

When she started to feel a little dizzy, she was tempted to put a hand on his arm for support. It was hard to tell if it was his nearness or the speed of the elevator that had produced the strange sensation. Luckily they reached their destination before she made a complete fool of herself and fell against him.

Terri expected the elevator door to open into another corridor. But as she was coming to find out, nothing had been as it seemed from the moment she'd heard the message about Richard on her answering machine.

In this case, the elevator served as the front door to a home like the kind you drooled over in an architectural magazine. She might as well have stepped into some heavenly villa on one of the Greek Islands. Rounded archways and white walls with area rugs and furnishings provided splashes of vivid color.

They stood in a stunning foyer. "How beautiful!"

"Let me show you around."

She took one look at his drawn features and shook her head. "I can do that myself. You're pale. Leave everything in the elevator," she said when he made a move to pick up her suitcase. "I'll get it. Right now you need to lie down. Let's go."

He studied her for a moment before starting down the hall on her right. The whole place was air-conditioned, bringing blessed cool to the interior.

"In there is the guest bedroom."

She followed him past that room to his bedroom, another spacious haven done in the same decor.

"While you're in the bathroom, I'll turn down your bed."

It was king-size with a Mondrian print-on-white quilt.

Paintings and dark hand-carved wood furniture provided the contrast to white walls.

When Ben emerged from the bathroom still dressed in the same clothes, she urged him to get on the bed where she'd propped some pillows. Without asking his permission, she removed his shoes and socks. A sigh slipped out of him, telling her she'd done the right thing.

"Just rest. I'll bring you something to eat."

As she hurried from the room to the elevator, she thought he might have called her name, but she kept on going. He needed food.

It didn't take long to carry the bags to the kitchen. She found it beyond the dining room, which adjoined the living room. Terri loved to cook and couldn't have been happier to discover the modern kitchen was an absolute dream with every convenience.

Broth might be all right for a drink, but her patient needed something more fortifying right now. She rummaged through the sacks until she found a can of beef stew whose contents she put in the blender. In a minute she poured the puree into a saucepan and warmed it on the stove.

With some more poking around, she found a tray. Eventually she'd loaded it with the stew, a can of peach nectar which she'd opened, a glass of water and a bottle of painkillers.

When she entered the bedroom, Ben's eyes were closed. But he must have smelled the aroma because his lids flew open at her approach.

"Let's hope this will help your weakness. You should have stayed in the hospital another day you know."

"I had to get out of there."

She understood, but she didn't tell him that.

As soon as he sat up straight, she put the tray on his lap. "Do you need a painkiller?"

He nodded.

"I'll open the bottle for you."

The second she put two pills on the tray, he popped them in his mouth and drank some water. Then he started in on the stew. She smiled to watch the way he practically gobbled it down.

"Ah-h…you'll never know," he whispered when it had disappeared.

"I'm glad you enjoyed it. There's more if you want it."

He darted her a glance. "How about in a half hour?"

"So it's going to be like that is it?"

His half smile turned her heart over. "I have a big appetite as you're about to discover. While I drink this nectar, why don't you bring me the blue folder on my desk."

Terri found it right away.

"Pull up a chair next to the bed. There's something I want to show you." When she'd done his bidding, he handed her an elaborate brochure. "I could tell in the car you were dying to ask questions. This should answer some of them."

For the next twenty minutes she became fully engrossed in a description of the ship and its purpose.

The Spirit of Atlantis *is a literal floating city that will travel the globe for years to come. Besides offering an international consortium of businesses, conference rooms, manufacturing plants and warehouse storage, everything is free of income, sales and duty tax.*

Families will live in beautiful residential homes they own outright. Other amenities are satellite TV and telephones, schools, a library, a first-class hospital, fire department, police department, duty free shopping centers, supermarkets, banks, post office, restaurants, cafés, theatres, chapels, a concert hall, recreational and gym facilities with a track, swimming pools, tennis courts, a handball court, beauty salons, a park, a florist, an airport and heliport to ferry passengers and guests to and from various coastal cities around the world.

The concept was mind-boggling. Terri turned to the section that showed the layout of the ship. Further on she read about the golf cart type vehicles used by residents to get around if they didn't want to walk everywhere.

She finally put the brochure down. When she lifted her eyes, she discovered that the mastermind behind this phenomenal enterprise had been watching her reaction with great interest.

"T-this is overwhelming," she stammered, still trying to take it in. "How long was it your dream before you turned it into reality? No—" She jumped to her feet and took the tray from him. "Don't answer that. Your throat needs more time to heal. I'm going to get settled in the other room, then I'll be back to check on you."

"Terri?"

"Yes?" she called to him from the doorway.

"Thank you. Tomorrow I'll take you to the place where the accident happened. I'm sorry that I didn't feel up to it today."

A wave of guilt washed over her before she slipped away to do some housekeeping chores. Since he'd appeared at her hotel room door this morning, she'd all but forgotten about Richard, let alone the reason that had brought her to Ecuador in the first place.

Ben clearly needed a lot of sleep because he didn't waken until six that evening. Knowing a liquid diet wasn't going to do it for him, she heated up the contents of some baby food for his dinner. Besides carrots and beans, she made mashed potatoes that would slither down his throat without effort.

When she took him the tray, he wolfed everything down in record time. After two helpings of potatoes which he praised, plus three bowls of ice cream, each a different flavor, he declared he was full. She gave him two more pills and told him to go back to sleep.

To her relief, the next time she peeked in on him, he was dead to the world. She supposed there was nothing like being home in your own bed. Careful not to make a sound, she put away the pajamas and robe she'd run through the washer and dryer. Worried that the room might be too cool, she covered him with the quilt and turned off his reading lamp.

After cleaning up the kitchen, she switched off lights and headed for the guest bedroom. In case he needed something in the night she purposely kept both their doors open.

Her shower felt good. When she'd prepared for bed, she wandered over to the window which gave out on a view of the coast in the far distance. She didn't know what floor they were on, but they had to be high up.

Normally you wouldn't think of a shipyard as being beautiful. But because it was night, the place looked exactly like a port city whose twinkling lights glinted on the water.

She rubbed her arms as if to remind herself she wasn't dreaming. It didn't seem possible she was on a floating city down in South America, getting ready to go to bed in a room next to a man who was neither her husband nor her fiancé.

Her thoughts flicked to Richard. The idea of working on a ship like this must have thrilled him as nothing else could have done. He'd probably dropped whatever he was doing back in the States to be a part of it.

Tomorrow Ben would supply the answers to questions about her ex-husband she hadn't yet asked. Terri sensed there was an unfavorable story to be told. Too bad it wouldn't come as any surprise to her.

Expelling a deep sigh, she climbed into the queen-size

bed. No sooner had she turned off her bedside light than the phone rang. Afraid it would waken Ben, she picked it up after the first ring and said hello.

"Terri?" a familiar male voice said her name.

"Parker?"

"It's nice to know you recognized me." He was a determined soul.

"If you were hoping to talk to your brother, he's asleep in the next room. I don't dare disturb him."

"I'm glad to hear that because it's you I wanted to talk to."

"I was asleep, too," she lied, not knowing how to put him off without hurting his feelings. But maybe it would have to come to that if he didn't take the hint soon.

"A word of advice. Don't let him boss you around. Ben's a notorious slave driver."

That made her mad. She sat up in the bed. "He should still be in the hospital."

"As you've found out, he lives by his own set of rules."

Yes. That's why he's such a remarkable man, her heart cried.

"I appreciate your interest, Parker, but I have to hang up now."

"Why? Is he calling for you again?"

"As a matter of fact I am," Ben whispered into the phone unexpectedly.

Terri's hand tightened on the receiver. Though she hated the fact that the call had disturbed her patient, she wasn't sorry he'd broken in on a conversation that was going nowhere.

"Goodbye, Parker," she said.

After hanging up the phone, she jumped out of bed and threw on a robe. Turning on the light in the hall, she made her way to Ben's bedroom. Halfway across the floor she heard the phone ring again. That meant her host had brought an abrupt end to the conversation with his brother.

"Do you want me to get it?"

"Please."

She picked up the receiver, ready to do battle if Ben's brother gave her any more trouble. "Parker? I'm sorry, but we can't talk to you right now. Maybe tomorrow. All right?"

"For your information, Mrs. Jeppson, this is Martha Shaw. I phoned the hospital and found out Ben had been released, so I'm assuming he's well enough to talk to me. I can't imagine what you're doing there with him. Put him on the line please."

"Just a minute."

Sucking in her breath, Terri covered the mouthpiece, then turned to Ben who looked far too appealing lying there in the semidarkness. His gaze trapped hers.

"Tell Martha I'm asleep."

Terri blinked. "How did you know it was she?"

"The accident has given me psychic powers."

He might mock, but she wondered if he and the other woman weren't in the middle of a lovers' quarrel. "She cares for you very much. Is there some kind of message I could give her so she won't stay upset?"

"No."

Terri had been around Ben long enough to know he meant what he said.

She lifted the receiver once more. "I'm afraid you'll have to call back in the morning, Ms. Shaw."

"I'll do better than that. Tell Ben I'll see him tomorrow." She banged down the receiver.

Crushed to think she would probably never be alone with Ben again after the other woman arrived, Terri slowly put the phone back on the hook.

"What happened to make you lose color like that?"

"Did I?" she half gasped. "I guess it was because she sounded very hurt. She said you could expect to see her tomorrow."

Ben cursed under his breath.

"I can understand her feelings. Ms. Shaw imagines I'm some kind of threat to her. Of course it's perfectly ridiculous, but she doesn't know that. Wouldn't it have been better if you'd at least whispered you loved her?"

The second the question came out of her mouth, she wished she hadn't asked it. His relationship with Martha Shaw was none of her business. Judging by the strange expression marring his features, she'd angered him.

Her deceased father used to tell her that her desire to fix every situation to make the world right was a wonderful character trait. But there were times it got her into trouble, so she had to be careful. Too bad she hadn't followed his advice just now.

"I'm sorry, Ben. Please forgive me for speaking out of turn. It's one of my worst faults."

"At least you called me by my first name. I believe we're making progress. Sit down on the chair, Terri. I want to talk to you."

She did his bidding, but she had a pit in her stomach.

"Where did you get the insane idea I was in love with Martha Shaw?"

His question filled her with so much joy, she could hardly concentrate on giving him an answer.

"When Parker drove me to Richard's apartment, her name came up in the conversation. I happened to make the comment that she was in love with you. Your brother asked me how I knew. I told him it was instinct. That's when he went very quiet and changed the subject."

She played with the end of her belt. "I—I just assumed that you and Ms. Shaw were involved in some kind of romantic relationship. Especially as she kept calling you at the hospital. When you refused to talk to her, I thought maybe you were having an argument of some kind. I didn't know…''

She heard a weary sigh escape his throat.

"Martha is Parker's ex-wife."

"What?" Terri almost fell off the chair.

"A long time ago she went to work as a secretary for my brother Creighton who now runs the oil company for Dad. On one of my trips home to Houston a few years ago, I happened to meet her and she made a play for me. Though she was attractive, I like to be the one who does the chasing and let her know I wasn't interested."

Whoa.

"The next thing I heard, Parker had fallen hard for her. I love my brother and didn't want to see him get hurt. When he told me he'd proposed to her, I should have told him about Martha. Instead I warned him off the institution of marriage. That was my fatal mistake. He just laughed at me.

"When his big day came, I made certain I had an emergency down here that prevented me from attending the wedding. It didn't take long for him to realize what I'd already found out. Martha was too self-absorbed to love anyone but herself. According to Mom and Dad, he did a lot of soul searching before he asked her for a divorce.

"The settlement was too generous of course. Even then she only agreed to give him his freedom as long as she could have her old job back with Creighton. My older brother didn't want any part of it. But he finally caved in to help speed up Parker's divorce with the proviso that Martha had to take back her maiden name."

After hearing Ben's explanation, there was no doubt in Terri's mind that Martha Shaw had fallen in love with the elusive bachelor of the Herrick family. Parker's ex-wife had never gotten over Ben. Terri could understand that better than any woman.

"I wish I'd known the truth before I blurted to your brother that I could tell she was in love with you. That must have hurt him terribly. I'm so sorry. What can I do?" she lamented.

"Nothing. You had no way of knowing Martha's history. I'm not so sure you didn't do Parker a favor. Since the divorce he has blamed himself that the marriage didn't work."

"So now he's going to blame *you?*" she blurted in agony.

"No, Terri. He knows my home has been here for the last eight years. If I don't miss my guess, your innocent observation may have helped him to see that she was never committed to their marriage. It has probably removed a burden of guilt he should never have felt in the first place.'

"I hope you're right." Her voice shook. Tears smarted her eyes. "How does she live with herself? Parker's a wonderful person. It was so cruel to marry him, and utterly unfair to you."

"That's all history. Right after the divorce, he flew down here and spent a month with me. We're closer than ever."

"That will change if he finds out she's coming to see *you* tomorrow."

"I hope she does."

"Why do you say that?"

"Because she'll be in for the biggest shock of her life. We'll discuss it in the morning."

All this talk had worn him out. He wanted to go back to sleep. She got up from the chair.

"Thank you for telling me the truth."

"You sound like it's the end of the world. It isn't. Just don't get any ideas about consoling Parker."

"The thought never crossed my mind."

"Maybe not consciously. But two people who've both lost a spouse already have something in common. Let's hope you're not still blaming yourself for a marriage that wasn't meant to be."

"I did at first," she admitted. "But after a while, I realized Richard fought the chains of marriage. From the little I heard about his aunt and uncle, they were pretty rigid. His parents died in a small plane accident. He never remembered them, and always resented the fact that life wasn't fair.

"Instead of enjoying his freedom until his thirties, he turned right around and married me after they died. I represented another cage of sorts."

"He was too immature and possibly too self-absorbed to know he'd won the prize. The same could be said of Martha. She lost a man who's one in a million."

"I agree."

Terri knew Ben meant Parker. But Terri also knew Martha could never see past Ben.

"Now my brother thinks he's in love again. You *do* have a quality that encourages a person to bare his soul. It's no wonder he can't leave you alone. I'm afraid drastic measures are called for."

She frowned. "What do you mean?"

"As I said, we'll discuss everything in the morning. Good night, Terri."

"Good night," she whispered.

When Terri looked up at the sky the next morning, thick cloud cover prevented any sunlight from breaking through. Ben had told her a storm was brewing. He suggested they go out to the accident site first thing, then come back for breakfast.

They walked to the starboard side of the ship. Two seamen at the landing helped them with life preservers before offering Terri assistance into the tender. Ben followed with his usual deftness.

He nodded to the seaman who started up the motor. Within seconds they sped away from the ship, then traveled parallel to it until they'd gone past the bow.

By now they'd left the protection of the inlet where the wind had picked up. Terri clung to the side of the boat as large swells in the open sea caused the tender to lift, then drop. Another minute and Ben made a hand signal for the seaman to cut the motor. His eyes swerved to Terri's.

"This is the approximate spot where the accident occurred. I had hoped to explain everything while we were out here, but the sea is too rough. After we return to the ship, I'll tell you the whole story."

Terri was glad he'd said that. Now that she'd seen the place where Richard had died, she wasn't sorry to go back to the ship. The elements were growing fierce.

"Thank you for showing me."

"It was the least I could do." He gave a signal to the seaman to turn them around and head back. Their boat rolled with the swells, not reaching safety any too soon for Terri. In the short time they'd been out, the sky had darkened to pitch and the wind had whipped up whitecaps.

The same two seamen relieved her of the preserver and helped her back into the ship. Ben wasn't far behind. On their way to the private elevator she said, "I have an idea that will save your voice.

"While I fix us breakfast, why don't you type out the explanation on the laptop I saw on your desk. It may take a while, but if you just use one finger, it shouldn't hurt your burn too much."

He flashed her a quick smile of approval. It dissolved her bones. She averted her eyes, afraid to stare at him any longer. They walked to his private elevator in silence.

On the way down to this deck, she'd found out he lived on the fifteenth floor. Terri still had a hard time believing any of this was real.

When they reached his condo, she hurried into the kitchen to fix their meal. Judging by the way he'd eaten yesterday, she figured he was ready for scrambled eggs, hot cooked cereal and juice.

Before long she breezed into his bedroom with the tray. "How's it going?"

He was seated at his desk. "I'm almost through."

"You sound like your voice is getting stronger. There's more deep tone than whisper. It's a wonderful sign."

"I have to admit I'm relieved."

"That's why you need to protect it for another day at least."

He had to be so thankful to be getting back to normal. While she waited for him to join her, Terri set two places at the table. In a minute he got up and brought her the laptop.

His gaze darted to the food. "You must have been reading my mind."

"I thought you were about ready for junior meals today."

His chuckle turned into laughter.

"Careful you don't pull out those stitches under your chin."

He sat down at the table. "It's okay, they're the dissolving kind."

Terri ate a bite of her eggs before she began reading the words at the top of the screen. The time had come to find out exactly what had happened on that fateful day.

On many occasions your ex-husband showed up for work late, or didn't report at all. More often than not he was hung over. The foreman gave him several chances to turn things around, but the same thing kept happening.

In order to fire him, the foreman had to go through my office first and obtain permission. Carlos looked into the situation and gave your ex-husband one final warning. But it was to no avail. At that point, Carlos brought the problem to my attention because I have the final say.

I looked over your ex-husband's work application. He'd listed his last work experience in Baton Rouge. I made a phone call. It turns out he'd left that job to come and work for my company. According to the man in charge there, Richard hadn't been very reliable and would probably have been let go before long.

It's my policy to give any man a chance to work and prove himself. There's nothing I dislike more than to fire an employee, especially if he has a family. Your ex-husband indicated he had a wife, Terri, his next of kin. He put his home address as Lead, South Dakota.

On the day in question, I waited until he was through with his work, then approached him on the ship. I told him I would run him to shore because I wanted to talk to him alone. He realized what was about to happen and became defensive.

Unfortunately there was a tropical storm further out at sea and we were feeling the effects of it. When I realized he hadn't put on his life preserver yet, I ordered him to get it on because we were in for a ride. He refused, so I turned the boat around and headed back to the ship. It was a good deal closer than the shore which you couldn't see.

To my horror, a speedboat traveling out of control suddenly came at us out of the darkness. Two young men without preservers who'd probably been on a joy ride in the storm crashed into us broadside, slicing the tender in two. Their bodies went flying.

One look at Richard and I realized he'd been knocked unconscious. I tried to reach him, but fuel had spilled from the tank, spreading fire. It separated us. I saw the others engulfed by flames before they slipped beneath the water. They never resurfaced.

I swam around frantically looking for Richard, but he was nowhere to be found. Three men were gone. I felt so damn guilty for being alive. The last thing I remembered was a fisherman pulling me into his boat. Before I blacked out, I remember crying out your name and begging him to get in touch with you.

"What a nightmare for you!" Terri cried. "Thank God you survived!" Without conscious thought she reached out to cover his hand. "Promise me you won't ever feel guilty again. If Richard hadn't refused to put on a life preserver, he would probably have lived. Like those young men, my ex-husband always did feel immortal."

He shook his head. "If I'd waited to fire him in Carlos's office at the dock, none of this would have happened. There've been several deaths because of heart attacks or natural causes, but until now I've always prided myself on the fact that the company has never had a drowning."

Terri jumped to her feet. "You can't go on living with 'what if's!' Obviously you were trying to do the right thing by letting him go when no one else was around. I admire you for sparing him any embarrassment or shame. It wasn't your fault he wouldn't wear a preserver, or that a speedboat ran into you. Accidents happen."

He eyed her solemnly. "According to Carlos, the police have determined that two Brazilians on holiday further down the coast were the ones who died. I've hired a diving service to search for the bodies. So far they haven't turned up anything. Carlos told me the coast guard believes it's a futile exercise at this point."

"That doesn't surprise me, Ben. Now that I've been out where the accident happened, I realize how deep and treacherous it is. The underwater current has probably swept them out to sea.''

''Can you live with that?''

Beneath the anguish, she heard something else in his voice.

''Of course I can! If you're laboring under some illusion that I'm still in love with Richard, then you haven't been listening to me. He killed my love years ago. Naturally I'm sorry he had to die this young, but it happened.

''The only way this will turn into a tragedy is if you allow guilt to taint your life. As Captain Ortiz said, you're a very important man. Besides all your many business connections, thousands of people depend on you for their livelihood. You mustn't let this eat at you.

''If there's anyone to feel sorry for, it's Juanita Rosario. She's the one who's in mourning, but I'm confident a new baby will help her to get over Richard. Now that I'm in possession of all the facts, I think I know why he pretended to be married before he came down here.''

While they'd been talking, Ben had finished his breakfast. He pushed himself away from the table and got to his feet. She sensed he was waiting for her explanation.

''Richard always liked women, but couldn't bear commitment. It probably saved him a lot of grief to tell Juanita he was married so she wouldn't have expectations he couldn't fulfill.''

Ben nodded. ''That thought had crossed my mind.'' She heard him expel a deep sigh. ''Tell you what—I promise not to feel guilty anymore if you'll let me help you plan a memorial service for him.''

''I'd love that,'' she said emotionally.

A gleam of satisfaction entered his incredible gray eyes. ''Good.''

''The only thing is, Mom and I already talked about it.

We think it should be held in Spearfish where he was born. She's been making the arrangements.''

"That makes perfect sense. I'll contact the captain of my company jet and we'll fly to South Dakota in the morning. By then the weather will be better.''

"Are you sure you can leave when you're this close to setting sail?''

His features hardened. "A man died under my watch. Anything else will have to be put on hold until he's had a proper service.''

"Thank you,'' she whispered.

Terri had felt a bond with this man from the beginning. Now she knew why.

She'd fallen in love with him.

It had happened without any volition on her part. What she felt for him was so all-consuming, she was in literal pain. Somehow Ben Herrick had stormed her heart, changing the tenor of her life forever.

Terrified he would divine her secret, she jumped up from the chair and started putting everything back on the tray. "Since you're still recuperating, now might be the best time for the surprise I've had planned for you.''

His lips twitched. Apparently her comment had pleased him. "Does it have to do with food?''

"I realize the thought of a big juicy steak never leaves your mind, but no— This is something entirely different. You have to lie down first.''

In a few long strides he reached the bed which had already been made up by someone in housekeeping. Once he'd settled back on top of the quilt, he flashed her a wicked smile. In navy sweats, he looked irresistible.

"How did you know I've been praying you'd give me another leg massage?''

Heat scorched her cheeks. "Wrong again.''

While he sat there scrutinizing her every move, she turned on the TV and VCR, then pressed play.

Pretty soon she heard him chuckle as *The Mummy* flashed on the screen. It had Spanish subtitles.

"As long as there's a storm outside, I thought this might be the perfect way to pass the time."

He eyed her for a long moment. "It *will* be perfect if you'll bring us some chocolate ice cream and join me."

Terri didn't need to be asked twice. She disappeared into the kitchen and fixed two heaping bowls for them. When she returned, he patted the side of the bed next to him.

Her heart skipped a beat as she handed him one of the bowls. Much as she would have loved to nestle close to him, she opted for the chair and began eating.

While he was absorbed with the movie, Terri was absorbed with him. When the phone rang, she noticed his dark brows furrow in displeasure. Maybe something was wrong aboard the ship. He put his spoon down and reached for the receiver with his free hand.

Realizing the TV could interfere with his conversation, she rushed over to the machines and turned them off. But she needn't have bothered because he'd already hung up.

"Is something wrong?"

His eyes narrowed on her features. "There won't be if you'll play along with me…"

CHAPTER SIX

THAT sounded rather cryptic.

Terri swallowed hard. She was so in love with Ben, she didn't see how she could deny him anything. Yet intuition told her to tread carefully.

He got up from the bed. "Forget I said anything. You're welcome to stay in here and finish the movie while I deal with Martha."

"She actually flew down here?" Terri was incredulous. "I mean, I know what she said, but I honestly didn't believe she'd be that brazen."

"One of the stewards just informed me she's on the lower deck waiting for permission to come up."

"How dare she show her face! What if Parker were here?"

"I suppose psychiatry has a name for it."

"Why doesn't your brother fire her?"

"He's afraid it will cause her to take Parker back to court for more money. My little brother is trying to run a productive cattle business, but her greed has made it difficult."

Terri's mind was reeling. "How would my help make any difference to a woman as driven as she is?"

"Since it's jealousy of you that brought her here in the first place, quite a lot, actually. In fact I have a hunch your cooperation will solve a problem that's been plaguing the Herrick family for a long time."

"Well, since you put it that way, I'll do whatever I can."

"You're sure?"

She flashed him a puzzled glance. "For an entrepreneur of your ilk, I'm surprised at your hesitation."

His white smile dazzled her. "I haven't heard the word 'ilk' used in ages."

"Your teasing is wasted on me. When I say I'll do something, you don't have to worry I won't follow through," she declared earnestly.

"I know that," he said in a solemn tone. "Come on." She followed him out of the room and down the hall. "Let's get this over with. I'll send the elevator for her."

"Where should I be when she arrives?"

"Why don't you go in the kitchen and fix us some drinks."

"All right."

With both ears listening for the sound of voices, Terri put ice in the tumblers and took three colas from the fridge. Grabbing some napkins, she placed everything on the tray.

Too bad she hadn't stopped by her room to put on more lipstick and brush her hair. She could have changed out of her jeans and blouse into something more formal. But it was too late now. A woman's voice carried through the rooms to the kitchen.

Terri picked up the tray and headed for the living room. She had to admit she was curious to meet the woman who'd married Parker to stay close to Ben. You never really knew about people until you met face-to-face. The Houston secretary who'd phoned Terri in the beginning had sounded so nice.

Ben saw Terri emerge from the dining room and urged her to join them. Her gaze switched from him to the woman seated at the end of the couch next to his chair. In a word, Martha Shaw was darling.

Of average height and weight, she'd swept her long brunette hair back in a ponytail. Her big brown eyes and dimples, that broad white smile—all those elements tended to remind Terri of the girl-next-door type. In an apple-green top and pants, she could see why Parker had been so attracted. Why any man would be. Ben appeared to have been the exception.

"We meet at last," Terri murmured. She offered his guest a drink.

"Yes." The other woman reached for a glass. "Who would ever have dreamed it was Ben lying there instead of your husband? I'm sorry to hear about his death."

"Thank you," Terri murmured. "I appreciated all your help making my travel and hotel arrangements so I could get down here without problem. I really couldn't have managed without you." She turned to Ben. "Would you like a drink?"

He reached for a glass. "Come on and sit down."

She put the tray on the coffee table and found another chair.

Martha's smile wasn't quite as bright as before. "I was just telling Ben that my boss, Ben's brother Creighton, allowed me to fly down to be of assistance until Ben has fully recovered."

She was a brilliant liar.

Terri had no idea what Ben expected her to say to that. "There's nothing like family support in a crisis."

"Or an irreplaceable office manager like Carlos," Ben interjected suavely.

Defeated on all fronts, the other woman stared pointedly at Terri. "How long do you plan to stay here?"

"I'm leaving for South Dakota in the morning."

"I see. Now that I've come, I'll be happy to help you with arrangements for your return flight."

Ben drained his glass and set it down on the table. "That won't be necessary. I've already taken care of everything."

"In your condition, you shouldn't have to be bothered."

"It's not a bother, Martha. Rather it's a privilege since I'm flying Terri to South Dakota to help her plan a memorial service for her ex-husband."

She choked on her drink. Her brown eyes fastened on Terri once more. "Ex-husband—you're divorced?"

"For a year. Richard lied about our marital status on his application. I can't tell you how surprised I was to get your message. In the first place, he and I had lost track of each other. When I heard he'd been in an accident in Ecuador, it completely threw me."

Martha looked furious.

Terri felt compelled to explain. "The only reason I didn't tell you I was divorced was that I thought maybe the Herrick Company only hired married people to work outside the States. I was afraid if I said something, it could get Richard into trouble at a time when he needed help the most."

"Why would you care?" The question summed up the other woman's shallow character.

Terri sucked in her breath. "Because being divorced didn't mean I wasn't concerned about his welfare. For a period of time, we shared a life. That has to count for something."

"I guess it all depends on the husband." Martha's brittle remark made Terri's heart go out to Ben's brother.

"Ben tells me you were once married to Parker, Martha. Even though you're divorced now, I'm sure if he were in dire trouble and needed your help, you'd give it because of what he'd meant to you in happier times."

"Maybe."

Terri couldn't let Martha's comment go. "When I went to see Richard's pregnant girlfriend and tell her he had died, Parker helped translate for me. He also gave her some of his own money on behalf the Herrick Corporation to help tide her over. Those were the actions of a truly kind person.''

Ben's searching gaze met Terri's. Obviously this was the first he'd heard about her outing with Parker.

''What I'm trying to say is, everyone has been wonderful throughout this whole, difficult ordeal. I want to thank you again, Martha, for making the situation easier for me at the beginning.''

''Of course.'' Her attention drifted to Ben. ''How soon will you be back from South Dakota?''

''I'm not sure.'' Ben got up and walked behind Terri's chair. Putting his hand on her shoulder he said, ''It will all depend on how soon Terri's willing to marry me and become my private secretary as well as my wife.''

A stunning silence followed.

Terri watched the blood drain out of Martha's face, even as her own heart turned over and over. She struggled for breath. A certain remnant of conversation flashed through her mind.

Is there something wrong?

There won't be if you play along with me...

Martha gripped the end of the sofa. ''You're getting married?'' She stared straight at Terri for verification.

Help.

A little while ago Terri had told Ben he could depend on her to follow through with whatever plan he had in mind. But for him to take things this far meant he was desperate!

''N-no one knows about it yet,'' Terri stammered. ''We have to get the memorial service behind us first.''

She felt a firm squeeze that sent warmth streaming through her sensitized body.

''So you see,'' Ben filled in, ''I won't be needing any assistance from other quarters. I'll phone Creighton and tell him I appreciated his willingness to let you fly down to be of help.''

''That won't be necessary.'' Martha sounded like she was a victim of shell shock.

Ben finally let go of Terri's shoulder. ''We were in the middle of a movie when you arrived, and would like to get back to it. I'll walk you to the elevator.''

Now that Terri had capitulated, she needed to act like a woman in love for as long as it took to get rid of Martha. It wouldn't be hard, not when Ben had become her whole world.

She jumped up from the chair and caught hold of his hand. ''You should be in bed. I'll see Martha out.''

He lowered his head and kissed Terri on the side of the neck, reducing her body to jelly. A word of goodbye to Martha and he left the living room.

Somehow Terri found the presence of mind to ask the other woman if she would like to use the guest bathroom before she left the ship.

''I don't think so.'' She marched to the foyer ahead of Terri and stepped inside the elevator.

''Have a safe trip back to Texas.''

The furious glitter in Martha's brown eyes was the last thing Terri saw before the door slid shut.

Without wasting any time, Terri headed for Ben's bedroom. He'd turned the movie back on and appeared to be enjoying it.

''She's gone.''

He pressed the pause button on the remote. ''My tactic worked.''

She could tell he was pleased, but his air of calm was mildly irritating when she could hardly breathe because her heart was pounding so hard.

''I agree it got her out of your hair. But she's going to go back and tell your brother that you and I are getting married. When your family finds out it's not true, she'll probably resort to other methods to pursue you. I'm afraid you just may have created a monster.''

''That all depends on you.''

''What do you mean?''

''In the hospital I made the decision that when this was all over, I was going to ask if you would come to work for me as my private secretary. I've never had one before, never saw the need for one.

''But there's a quality about you that has caused me to change my mind. I found out right away you're a person who lights her own fires. You're unique in this world. Someone who would be invaluable to me now that my dream is becoming reality.''

She clasped her hands together. ''Coming from a business tycoon like yourself, I'm very flattered, of course, but—''

''I'm not finished.''

''I'm sorry.''

''No, you're not,'' he brushed off her apology, ''but that's all right. For several days I've been asking myself what it would take to lure you away from your creature comforts back in the Black Hills.''

Every word that fell from his lips made her pulse accelerate.

''I can promise you more problems to fix on this ship than you've had to tackle at the chamber of commerce. All you have to do is name your own salary. I can offer you a lifetime of security and benefits. Free visits for your family, time off to visit them. The opportunity to see the world many times over. But something tells me none of that would be enough for you.''

''Well, thank you.''

A deep chuckle ensued. ''I'm not through. What makes you so necessary to me, so powerful in an invisible way, is that feminine part of you which knows how to deal with people. You ooze with compassion. But I recognize that side of you will never feel complete without a husband and children.''

She sank down in the nearest chair. He knew her far too well, and no wonder. During those first couple of days, she'd bared her soul to him in an attempt to pull him from the depths of his misery. She'd told him things she'd never admitted to another soul.

''In my clumsy way, which is a result of my being a bachelor these many years, I'm asking you to marry me.''

Dear God.

''You don't have to give me your answer right now. In fact I'd prefer you wait until the service for your ex-husband is over and you can concentrate.''

She got up from the chair, unable to sit still. ''I think you've been using your voice way too much and need to rest it.''

''There've been several women in my life,'' he persisted as if she hadn't said anything. ''Naturally there have. But I always had this dream driving me. It prevented me from putting down roots because I knew I couldn't be the kind of husband they needed.

''However these last few days have forced me to realize my life has entered a new phase. Your presence has crystallized my thinking. I find that the thought of going on alone brings me little pleasure.''

She cocked her head. ''What about love?''

''We've both known it before,'' he came back reasonably. ''Both of us have experienced first love, the first throes of passion, the excitement and mystery of what goes on between a man and woman. You've known what it's like to be pregnant and carry a baby inside you.''

Terri averted her eyes.

"Are you afraid that if you got pregnant again you would miscarry?"

After a brief hesitation she nodded.

"That would explain why you feel so anxious for Juanita."

Hot tears trickled from her eyes. "It's horrible to go through the experience of losing your baby alone." Her voice shook. "You feel so empty. And then not to be able to hold on to the man who helped to create that little life because he's not around, and doesn't want to be—"

She broke off, burying her face in her hands to get control of her emotions. Finally she lifted her head. "I'm sorry."

"Don't ever apologize for your emotions, Terri. They make me feel closer to you than ever. We already know we have this rare mental chemistry that practically allows us to read each other's minds. Between us there's respect and humor. And I believe loyalty.

"Those are precious ingredients that could form the basis for a solid marriage. What's to say that given time we wouldn't find love with each other?"

He'd left out desire.

It was all very well to talk about everything else, but without that one vital ingredient, there could be no passion. No excitement. No driving force. No babies.

Her desire for him had already reached an explosive level. But if he never felt the same way...

Maybe he *couldn't* feel that way. Maybe that lack in his psyche was the reason why he'd been able to stay a bachelor all this time.

She began to suspect that what she and Parker had talked about was true. The accident had made Ben vulnerable. For once in his adult life he'd experienced helplessness. For a short period of time he'd been forced to rely on someone else. That someone had happened to be Terri.

But these were early days. Give him another week to recover and he might be in a very different frame of mind. He probably knew that, which was why he'd told her not to give him an answer until after the memorial service. A shrewd businessman like him knew how to leave his options open.

"You make a compelling case. I'll think about it." But that's *all* I'll do, her heart cried.

"There's more. Parker thinks he has a chance with you. So does Carlos. All that either of them is waiting for is an opportunity to find out.

"If you become my wife, those problems will disappear. Furthermore I'll have the assurance that you won't be leaving me in the lurch at a future date to marry someone who could never appreciate you the way I do."

Stop, Ben. You're making me want it too much, want you too much.

He turned on his side. "I don't know about you, but all this talk has made me hungry again. The next time you feel the urge to go to the kitchen, I wouldn't mind a grilled cheese sandwich."

She gathered the empty bowls and put them on the tray. "According to the instructions Sister Angelica sent home, you can't have a sandwich until tomorrow. How about an omelet? I'll go heavy on the cheese."

"That'll taste good with about a half gallon of milk."

"I'm afraid you'll have to do with a quart," she retorted.

"When you come back, I'll turn on the movie. We were just getting to the good part."

"Don't wait for me," she called over her shoulder. "I've seen it before."

"But it won't be the same without you."

He shouldn't have said that. Especially if there was any chance that he really meant it...

"...so we thank thee for the life of Richard Jeppson. Though he is lost to us now, we know we will see him again when all will rise in the resurrection of our Lord. Amen."

Following the pastor's uplifting eulogy, the congregation sang a closing hymn. Terri was gratified to see that the small chapel had filled to capacity. A lovely tribute had been paid, not only to Richard, but to the aunt and uncle who'd raised him.

Holding a memorial service in Spearfish had been the right thing to do, but she couldn't forget the exciting man seated several rows behind her and her family.

Thanks to Ben's generosity, the church overflowed with flowers. He'd also made arrangements for a tombstone to be placed in the same cemetery plot where Richard's parents and aunt and uncle were buried.

For that gesture he'd won the praise of Terri's mother. She wouldn't hear of him going to a motel. Instead she insisted he be a guest at the Jeppson home in Lead. Her invitation prevented Terri from giving into the temptation of letting him stay at her apartment.

Over the three day period Ben had treated her like a cherished sister. He'd charmed Beth who became a constant visitor. Terri couldn't blame her. He was so attractive and fascinating, he had their family mesmerized.

No one wanted to see him fly back to Ecuador. Particularly not Terri who'd feared he'd changed his mind about wanting a private secretary, let alone a wife.

Ben didn't ache for her the way she did for him. That was why he hadn't broached either subject since they'd been in South Dakota.

When the noonday service came to an end, she purposely chatted with old friends and acquaintances in an effort to keep her distance from Ben.

"Honey?" Her mother put a hand on her arm. "I'm going to drive back to Lead with Beth and Tom. As soon as you and Ben get there, we'll have lunch."

"He's planning to leave for South America today, Mom."

"If I know him, he won't say no to a meal first."

Ben had been around long enough for her mother to figure that out. Since the swelling in his throat had subsided, he was able to eat whatever he wanted and couldn't seem to get enough.

Terri gave her parent a hug. "It was a wonderful service. Thanks for everything, especially for being you." Her voice quivered.

"Honey—what's wrong?"

"Nothing. I guess I'm feeling a little emotional."

"Then don't let him get away," her mother whispered. *She knew!*

"Terri?" Ben's voice had come back. His deep timbre resonated to every cell in her body. "Is there anything else I can do to help?"

In a hand-tailored gray silk suit, he looked so gorgeous she didn't dare give him another glance. Otherwise she'd end up feasting her eyes on him and make an utter fool of herself.

She moved away from her mother. "No, thank you. Shall we go?"

Terri started down the aisle ahead of him. After stopping outside the doors to talk to a few more well-wishers, she headed for the parking lot. Thankful to reach the car ahead of him, there could be no argument about who would drive.

She'd driven them to Spearfish in her Honda Civic. Normally she would have enjoyed letting him take the wheel.

But the doctor had said he should wear his arm in a sling for another two weeks at least. Thus she'd insisted on being the chauffeur.

Over the last three days they'd packed in quite a bit of sightseeing around the Black Hills. Time had passed so quickly, she couldn't believe it was about to come to an end. The knowledge that he was on the verge of leaving had plunged her into such a depressed state, it felt as if she was in mourning.

"Terri?" They'd just entered Lead. "Is there a reason why you haven't taken me to your apartment yet?"

The unexpected question seemed to have come out of nowhere. It caught her off guard.

"We've been so busy, there hasn't been time."

"We have time now."

Her heart jumped to her throat. "Mom has lunch waiting. After you're through eating, we'll need to get you to the airport in Rapid City."

"The pilot will be ready whenever I decide to leave."

"I don't think going to my place is a good idea." Terri continued toward her destination. She pulled into the driveway of her mom's house behind Tom's car.

Tension crackled between them as she turned off the ignition.

"Is that because you've decided to marry me, but you're afraid I'll try to make love to you before you're ready?"

What? "N-no!"

If anything, Terri was afraid he *wouldn't* try. *That's* what had stopped her. She shook her shook her head. "You've misunderstood me."

"I don't think so. Credit me with the sense to know this isn't the time or place. You've just put your ex-husband to rest. My interest in seeing the apartment where you knew so much unhappiness stems purely from the desire to know more about you. If sex were all I was after, the subject of marriage would never have been raised.''

Terri couldn't believe it.

Ben hadn't changed his mind.

He really was offering her marriage.

''I thought I'd made it clear we'll take things as they come and see what develops, but rest assured I live in the hope of one day enjoying every aspect of marriage with you, including children.''

''I'm not the best bet in the world on that score,'' she said in a haunted whisper.

''Since I haven't tried to father a child before, I guess neither of us can predict the future. But no matter what happens, I'll be there for you, Terri,'' he vowed fiercely.

Coming from Ben, she knew he meant it.

''Have I averted your fears on that score enough to tell your family our happy news? I'd like you to fly back with me today. We've a wedding to plan before we sail. Once we're underway, there'll be more work for us than I trust even your extraordinary imagination can conceive.''

Her heart thundered in her chest. After her first marriage had failed, only a fool would rush in a second time *knowing* he wasn't in love with her. It would be a marriage of convenience. But the thought of losing him, of never seeing him again...

''Do ship's captains still marry people at sea?''

Something flickered in the recesses of his eyes. ''Not unless they're a clergyman, too. Happily, Captain Rogers of the *Atlantis* was a naval chaplain and still retains his ecclesiastical authority.''

Maybe she was dreaming.

''The chapel on the first floor of the ship will accommodate our families nicely.''

''I'm afraid mine wouldn't be able to come, Ben. They don't have passports.''

"I have a government friend who will grant them temporary visas. What else is on your mind?"

"My boss."

"I feel sorry for the poor devil. He'll never be able to replace you."

Terri's mouth turned up at one corner. "He's not a poor devil."

"He will be when he hears the news."

She took a deep breath. "Won't your family be shocked?"

"It's guaranteed."

"When will you tell them?"

Their glances collided. "Is there any doubt in your mind they already know?"

"I suppose not." Martha had been furious. And hurt.

"Parker is probably in mourning as we speak."

Flame licked her cheeks. "Don't be ridiculous."

"What else are you worried about?" he drawled.

"I have an apartment to vacate."

"That's easy. With one phone call we can hire movers to pack. I'll send a company plane to transport everything to the ship."

The man moved with the speed of light. It caused her mind to run in a dozen different directions all at the same time.

"Beth and Tom need a second car. I could give them mine."

"Speaking of needs, you've reminded me that you'll have to bring along a birth certificate to get the application process started on your passport."

"I think Mom still has the original in a scrapbook somewhere."

He leaned closer. "She's waving to us from the front porch. Before we go in, there's one more thing to do. Give me your left hand so I can put this on.'' His voice sounded husky.

Out of the corner of her eye she saw something glint. Within seconds he'd pushed home a breathtaking diamond solitaire set in gold onto her ring finger. Terri's body trembled so hard, the different facets kept picking up the light, revealing a heart of fire to match the one blazing inside her.

''Terri? Ben?'' Captain Archibald Rogers of the *Atlantis* stood in front of them looking splendid in his white uniform.

''The day after tomorrow this great ship will undertake its maiden voyage. People around the world will laud it as a truly momentous occasion. They will say it is something unique in the annals of engineering, *miraculous* in the history of mankind's achievements.

''But as great as that will be, something more glorious is about to take place right now. Family, friends and business associates from near and far have assembled to witness the joining of you two fine, worthy people in the sacred bonds of holy matrimony. You are about to become a family, the mainspring of civilization.

''When a man and woman honor this hallowed institution, there can be no greater bond on earth, no greater haven, no greater refuge, no greater joy.

''In order for this precious state to exist forever, there's only one thing you need to ask yourself every day of life, Ben.

''What can I do for my wife today? Then do it!

''Terri? All you need to ask yourself every day is, what can I do for my husband? Then do it!

''When a husband and wife care more for each other than themselves, no power on earth can destroy that love which is blessed.

"Ben? Please take hold of Terri's hand and repeat after me."

She felt his strong, firm grasp capture hers. Afraid to meet his gaze, she kept her eyes on his lips. "I, Benjamin Herrick, promise to take thee, Terri Jeppson, for my beloved wife…"

As he repeated the words of the time-honored ceremony, Terri vowed she was going to do everything in her power to be such a wonderful wife, he would *have* to fall in love with her. But until that miracle happened, she had more than enough love for both of them.

"Terri? Repeat after me."

"I, Terri Jeppson, take thee, Benjamin Herrick, for my beloved husband…"

She could hear her voice tremble as she said the words. Ironically Ben's voice had been deep and strong when he'd spoken his vows. Gone was the mysterious stranger who'd whispered to her in agony from his hospital bed.

This man stood tall and resplendent in a formal midnight-blue suit with a gardenia in his lapel. He'd dispensed with the sling.

"You may now exchange rings. You first, Terri."

She pulled the wedding band made of Black Hills gold off her middle finger and put it on the ring finger of his left hand. To her relief it seemed to fit.

"Now you, Ben."

Her heart slammed into her ribs as he produced a wide gold band from his pocket and slid it next to her engagement ring.

"Symbols look beautiful, but they mean nothing without the backing of pure love. Therein lies the magic and the power of the union you have entered into at this hour.

"By the authority invested in me through the church, I now pronounce you husband and wife.

"Ben—you're not a man known for your patience when

you want something badly. Today I must commend you for your restraint this far into the service. You may now kiss your bride—for as long as you like.''

A chuckle rippled through the congregation.

''Do your best,'' Terri's new husband whispered.

She spied a devilish gleam of silver in his eyes before he lowered his mouth to hers.

Most people's first kiss was done in private. Hers, of course, had to be in front of a captive audience. But nothing about the situation with Ben had ever conformed to the norm.

He'd taken the captain's advice and seemed in no hurry to end the fun. For the benefit of their onlookers, Terri decided to get into it. At least that was the lie she told herself as she began kissing him back.

Then something changed. With infinite gentleness, he relinquished her mouth. Maybe it was a trick of light, but she thought he looked pale beneath his tan.

''You're in pain!'' she cried softly. ''I knew you should have worn your sling.''

''I'll be all right.''

But he wasn't all right! The more she thought about it, the more she feared something else had prompted such a drastic change in him. Like maybe the fact that she'd kissed him back?

Dear God—did Ben think she'd used their wedding kiss to wring a response from him he wasn't prepared to give yet? A response he might never feel? What had he said, maybe love would come to them one day?

''Family and friends,'' the captain spoke up, oblivious to her turmoil. ''Please rise. May I present Mr. and Mrs. Benjamin Herrick. If you'll join them in the anteroom for the wedding feast, you can offer them your congratulations and take all the pictures you want.''

Beth handed Terri the sheath of long-stemmed Texas

bluebonnets she'd been holding for her. Just as quickly, Ben put his arm around her waist and fairly swept her past the pews filled with smiling guests. But their faces were a blur. Already her wedding day had been shattered, and they hadn't even made it out of the chapel yet!

CHAPTER SEVEN

BEN'S father was the first person in line to give Terri a hug.

"You have no idea how happy you've made this family, especially my wife. She calls you Ben's savior. That son of ours has needed the gentling of a woman for years now. Do you know you're a vision in that dress, it matches your beautiful eyes? If Ben hadn't grabbed you, Parker would have. Welcome to the family."

His kindness moved her to tears. "Thank you, Mr. Herrick. You've all been wonderful."

"Honey?"

"Mom!" She let go of Ben's father to embrace her mother.

"You look like an angel."

"You always say that," Terri scoffed.

"Your husband thinks so, too. He hasn't taken his eyes off you since you walked into the chapel on Tom's arm."

All is not as it seems, Mom.

Beth clamored for her space. She threw her arms around Terri. "Richard could never measure up. Thank heaven Ben came into your life. If you want my opinion, it was all meant to be."

Terri had thought so too. Until that kiss...

"Name the first one after me," Beth whispered before the rest of the Herrick clan descended.

Creighton was every bit as charming as his brothers. Parker came at the tail end.

He stared at her for a long moment. "I never stood a chance, did I."

Her heart swelled with tenderness for him. "Parker—after my divorce I didn't think I'd get a second chance. I wasn't even sure I was entitled to one. What happened between your brother and me is something I really can't explain."

"You don't have to," he said. "It's called love. You two found the genuine article. Give me some time to get over the pain and I'll be happy for you."

Terri didn't know if she could take much more of this.

"You'll find true love too, Parker. I know you will."

His lips broke into that captivating smile. "How about a kiss to hold me until then?"

She thought it would be a simple buss on the cheek. To her surprise, he found her mouth and kissed her warmly.

"That was for Ben," he teased after letting her go. "Just to remind him he'd better be good to you, or there'll be hell to pay."

Suddenly she caught sight of her new husband who must have seen their embrace. His eyes had narrowed. Parker may have done it in fun, but Terri had the unsettling sensation that *she* was going to hear about it later.

"Mrs. Herrick?"

She swung around to discover Captain Ortiz.

"I'm so glad you could come to the wedding."

"I was honored to be invited. It is a pleasure for me to see happiness rise out of tragedy. Congratulations."

"Thank you, Captain. My heart goes out to the families of those two young men who died with Richard. Ben and I sent flowers."

"As I told you before, you have a generous nature. Perhaps too generous."

"What do you mean?"

"Juanita Rosario has phoned my office at least four times asking how she can get in touch with you. It's a good thing you'll be sailing soon. Enjoy your honeymoon.''

There wasn't going to be one, but Captain Ortiz didn't know that. In fact he had no idea how precarious things were with Ben right now, or how worried she was about Juanita.

Terri had told the other woman to reach her through the captain if there was an emergency. Unfortunately he'd made it clear he didn't approve of her giving Juanita money.

''Thank you, captain. Please stay and eat with us.''

''I won't say no.''

Carlos was next in line. His dark eyes sparkled with mischief. ''I didn't think there was a woman who could bring Ben to his knees. You've accomplished the impossible. Don't ever change. The boss needs you. Congratulations.''

Coming from the man Ben trusted with his life, those words warmed her clear through. ''Thank you, Carlos. I guess I don't have to tell you what your friendship means to my husband.''

Behind Carlos she could see several dozen business associates of Ben's who with their wives would be living on the *Atlantis*. They'd flown in from as far away as Hong Kong and Australia.

''Mrs. Herrick? May I offer my congratulations. I'm Rolf Meuller, one of the directors on your husband's board. I represent the Swiss Banking Consortium located in Zurich.'' He had a strong German accent.

''You're just the man I wanted to meet, Mr. Meuller. Between you and me, how deep in the red is he? A wife needs to know these things.''

The man with the steel-rimmed glasses threw back his head and laughed so hard, he had to remove them to wipe his eyes.

* * *

Ben counted four down so far: Parker, Carlos, Captain Ortiz and Rolf.

Another ten minutes and he saw his entire board of directors succumb to his bride's fatal charm. One by one they toppled like pins in a bowling alley following a direct strike.

Everything would have been all right if she hadn't kissed him back. *Lord,* she came close to giving him cardiac arrest. It was the one imponderable he hadn't expected.

He'd told Terri to do her best. But he hadn't expected her to comply with a response that left him trembling with desire.

After Ben had told her she could trust him, that they'd take each day as it came and see what happened, he couldn't go back on his promise. At the time, he'd meant what he'd said. He'd thought he could handle it.

But that was before Terri's kiss had swept him away. From now on he would have to live with the memory of her luscious mouth opening to the pressure of his. The time-worn cliché "invitation to paradise" was no longer laughable.

Ben had made his first mistake. *Hell.* Now he didn't know if her response had been playacting from start to finish, or if she'd experienced a genuine burst of passion she'd been helpless to fight. He'd sell his soul to know the truth, but it was too soon.

For one thing, how could he be sure that certain memories of making love with her ex-husband didn't still fit into the equation somewhere? Though Ben was ready to make a baby with her tonight, he'd assured her she had nothing to fear from him.

Somehow he was going to have to keep his hands off her until enough time had passed that she'd put the past away for good and felt totally comfortable with him. There'd be no wedding night for him tonight. That miracle would have to be put off for a week or two. Beyond that he wasn't making any more promises to himself.

While he'd lost his appetite, his bride appeared to be ravenous. Throughout their wedding feast she sparkled and laughed. Each time there was a toast, she entertained their guests with her inimitable wit.

Soon everyone was calling for them to give speeches. He supposed it was time to get his over with. It was in a foul temper that he rose to his feet.

"Terri and I want to thank everyone for being here to share this day with us. For a woman who's terrified of mummies, I have to admit I'm shocked she agreed to marry me."

The room exploded with laughter.

"She was there for me throughout my ordeal in the hospital. In the dark hours of the night while she came up with astonishing ways to entertain me, I realized I wanted her in my life for good.

"As most of you know, I've never had a wife or a private secretary. By some miracle, I now have both. They're seated at my side. Terri? Stand up and say something to the crowd. They're sick of me."

Everyone clapped and cheered.

Inside, Terri was dying. There'd been no mention of love in Ben's short speech. She'd had no right to expect it. What a fool she was for wanting something so totally out of reach.

If she were wise, she would be thankful for what he could freely give her and make the best of it. He wanted a secretary? She'd give him more than he bargained for.

Terri pushed herself away from the table and stood up.

"I'm afraid my poor husband doesn't know that every woman who's a wife, is already a private secretary."

The females in the room broke into laughter first. Then there was clapping. She waited until it quieted down.

"For my first order of business, I'm eliminating that title and creating a new one. From now on I'll be officially known on the *Atlantis* as the new head of the chamber of commerce. That is, if it's all right with my husband." She looked around at him, intercepting his enigmatic gaze.

"Do I have a choice?"

Their guests collapsed with laughter once more.

"You see how sweet he is? In case some of you didn't know, until a week ago I worked for the chamber of commerce in South Dakota. It's the work I do best. That umbrella will allow me much greater scope than the duties of a secretary.

"When Ben let me read the brochure, I noticed right away that the chamber of commerce was missing from the list of businesses. The *Atlantis* is a city, and every city needs a chamber. With so much on my husband's mind, I'm sure it was an oversight."

Some of his directors laughed outloud and burst into applause.

"Fortunately I can now troubleshoot problems of that nature for him. Already I've observed a few other things which will need addressing, but not today.

"Today is our wedding day. I want all of you to know I'm married to the most wonderful man I've ever known. Every woman should be so blessed. Thank you for celebrating with us."

As soon as Terri sat down, the captain of the ship took charge. "There will be dancing in the Blue Grotto Lounge on A deck specially arranged for this occasion. Before we go, let us lift our glasses in a final toast to our illustrious couple."

He beamed at them. "My wife just said she hopes that all your troubles will be little ones. Cheers."

Terri kept smiling, but inside her heart was breaking. Even if theirs became the normal marriage he'd alluded to, she was terrified she'd never be able to carry his baby the whole nine months.

Ben's arm went around her waist. "Everything in time," he whispered, displaying his uncanny ability to know what was going on in her mind. "This will be our first experience dancing together. I'm looking forward to it. Shall we go? Everyone's waiting for us."

She gathered the bluebonnets which had been a surprise gift from Ben and left the room on his arm. Outside the lounge where the ship's photographer took more pictures of them standing with their families, the unmistakable sounds of a Latin band playing salsa vibrated through her nervous system.

Soon her husband was drawing her through the doors to the dance floor. He pulled her into his arms. At this point her senses were uncontrollably alive. The exciting music only served to heighten her awareness of him.

Some of the couples were expert Latin dancers. She was relieved Ben didn't try to do anything spectacular. He simply moved her around, but even in that there was grave danger she'd give herself away with the motions of their bodies touching and swaying back and forth.

For the next fifteen minutes she struggled to keep a little distance between them. Thank heaven for the flowers she'd insisted on holding even though he'd suggested she put them down somewhere.

She finally lifted her eyes to his. "They won't last very long. I want to enjoy them as long as possible."

He studied her for a breathless moment. "In that case, why don't we slip away and put them in water. Everyone in the room is wondering how soon we're going to start our honeymoon. We might as well do our disappearing act now and give them a thrill.''

For an exit line it was brilliant. But she had no illusions he was dying to whisk her off to some private place and make love to her.

''That was easy,'' he said as soon as the door to his private elevator closed. ''Now that we're truly alone, tell me what you and Captain Ortiz were talking about. Did he say any bodies had been found?''

If anyone could hear their conversation right now, they wouldn't have a clue she and Ben had barely exchanged their wedding vows.

''No. In a word he said he was glad that despite the tragedy, something good had come out of it. He wished us every happiness in our marriage.''

Since Terri feared Ben might side with the captain when it came to giving Juanita money, she decided to leave that part out.

''That was nice of him.''

The elevator came to stop and the door opened to the condo. *Their* condo now. Wedding presents were piled high in the foyer. Terri could barely make her way through them to the living room.

She whirled around. ''It was a beautiful wedding, Ben. Everything a bride could wish for. Thank you for a perfect day. Your family's wonderful.''

''So is yours.''

He was trying to undo his tie. She reached up and helped him to ease it off along with his jacket.

He trapped her gaze. ''I noticed Parker consoling himself with the greatest of pleasure.''

Her pulse tripped over itself. ''He hoped you'd notice that kiss. I'm pretty crazy about that brother of yours. I hope he finds his equal one day soon.''

"So do I…" His voice trailed. "Creighton had some news."

"Oh, yes?"

"He fired Martha. Apparently he told her that if she tried to make any more trouble for Parker, he'd sue her for leaving Houston and using a company plane without his permission to fly down."

"So that's how she got here so fast!" Terri was aghast. "I'm glad he got rid of her, for *all* your sakes."

"It's the best wedding present he could have given us. What would you like to do now?"

"Open presents on your bed."

"Why in there?"

"Because you look tired. I happen to know you're in pain. Why don't we both change. You need to get that arm back in the sling. I'll bring some tablets."

"All that sounds good except the presents."

"Then we'll worry about them another day. I happen to have another surprise for you anyway."

She must have said the right thing. Something ignited in the depths of his eyes. "Don't take too long."

He'd sounded like he'd really meant it.

One thing she did know. He'd sought her companionship from the very first. As long as that never changed, she would nurse the hope that one day he'd show her he wanted more…

Terri's family had given her a lovely nightgown and matching peignoir, but she couldn't wear them around Ben. So it was back to the nightgown and robe she'd brought with her the first time. With a little rummaging, she found a certain video and stuffed it in her pocket.

In the kitchen Terri pulled a vase from the cupboard over the microwave. She filled it with water, then arranged the bluebonnets which had held up amazingly well.

After putting two pills in her other pocket, she headed

for Ben's bedroom with everything including a glass of water. Once she'd set the vase down on the table, she walked over to him. He'd gotten under the covers. "Here you go."

While he swallowed his tablets, she noticed he was wearing a new pair of pajamas in a coffee shade. And here she'd thought navy was his best color...

Needing to stay busy and out of trouble, she made an adjustment to his sling. When he'd finished drinking, she took the glass and put it back on the table.

"When are you going to give me my surprise?"

Terri eyed him provocatively. "Captain Rogers was right about your impatient streak." She pulled the video out of her pocket and put it in the machine. "This is Beth's wedding present to us."

The second *The Invisible Man* appeared on the screen, he chuckled.

"Can you believe she found it?"

"Come and watch it with me." Like déjà vu, she watched him pat her side of the bed, as if it were the most natural thing in the world.

It would be ridiculous for her to sit on a chair now. She was his wife after all.

Trying to act as nonchalant as possible, she walked over to the bed and lay down with her head at the foot. It felt so good to relax, she let out a deep sigh and rested her cheek on her arms. The old Hollywood film was great, but after a few minutes her eyelids started to droop.

"Your idea for establishing a chamber of commerce was brilliant. But your mention of several oversights has got me curious."

His comment brought her back to consciousness. She sat up. "You don't want to watch the movie?"

"I did watch it. I loved it."

"You mean it's *over?*"

"I'm afraid you slept through the whole thing."

"You're kidding!" She glanced at her watch. Two hours had passed. He was right. "Did I snore?"

Ben burst into laughter, the kind that came from deep down inside. "I'll never tell."

"I *did!*"

"If that's your only secret, you have no worries."

Oh, yes, I do. What if she'd talked in her sleep? What if she called out his name in longing?

"Which oversight do you want to hear about first?" She half grumbled the question.

"Whichever one you deem the most important."

"They're *all* important."

"Go on."

She bit her lip. "Are you sure you want to talk about this right now?"

He eyed her frankly. "What better time?"

Right.

"Your brochure talked about family living. I didn't see a veterinary hospital listed."

"The board voted against having pets on the ship."

"But most families have one. Why is the board against the idea?"

"Because there are a lot of rules and laws about animals. Quarantine procedures."

"Are there women on your board? I didn't meet any today."

A long silence followed before he said no.

"Well, that explains it. The men didn't want to be bothered. That's one of the reasons you need a chamber of commerce to make certain all services are offered. I'll look into the details and present a proposal at your next meeting. They probably didn't want a day care center, either."

"The subject never came up."

"Does that mean you have an age limit for children?"

"They have to be in high school."

"Really? I didn't see that in the brochure."

"A list of rules accompanies every brochure. I just don't happen to have one on my desk at the moment."

"Won't there be a problem if one of the mothers finds herself pregnant after thinking she was through?"

"If that should arise, the condo will have to be sold."

"Just supposing you and I were to have children. Would I have to live away from the ship?"

"Of course not."

"So there's one rule for the directors, but not for everyone else?"

"These directors have invested billions of dollars. That gives them rights."

"Then I think your dream could be destined for failure down the road."

"Would you care to explain that remark?" Though he'd asked the question in a civil enough way, she'd heard the underlying steel in his tone.

"This may be a floating city, but it needs babies and old people so it won't feel like some governmental experiment in outer space.

"I noticed there was no nursing home listed. What will happen if someone is diagnosed with Alzheimers and needs round-the-clock care? Or is there a rule that at sixty-five you have to sell your condo?"

His face closed up. She'd made him angry.

"I'm sorry, Ben. I didn't mean to get so carried away, but you did ask. I'm only giving my input from a woman's point of view. Have you presold all the condos?"

"No."

"Are sales up or down?"

"They're coming along."

"Maybe they would move faster if you didn't have those limitations. I know if I had the kind of money it took to buy a condo on the *Atlantis,* I wouldn't consider it if you couldn't have babies and pets. Without them it would feel like a giant country club. One night out is fun, but not a steady diet.''

His eyelids lowered to half-mast. ''Does this mean I can expect you to leave the ship for long periods of time?''

She got up from the bed. ''No. Of course not. I'm your wife and agreed to be your working assistant. I'll stand by you no matter what.''

Shadows darkened his face. ''Meaning even if I lose my shirt on this venture?''

''No!'' Terri groaned in pain. ''That's not what I said. You're twisting my words. How can you even ask that?'' she blurted in pain.

Devastated because her outspoken remarks had hurt him, she realized she'd ruined what had been the most beautiful day of her life. Somehow she had to make him understand it hadn't been intentional.

''Only a few hours ago I vowed to stay with you for better or worse, for richer, for poorer, in sickness and in health. If you think I made them lightly, then you don't know me at all.''

Heavy tension crackled between them like a live wire.

''After we're at sea I'll call a board meeting,'' he murmured. ''You'll be first on the agenda. Tell them what you've just told me.''

''I—I don't want to alienate them right off.''

He made a strange sound. ''You had them eating out of the palm of your hand a few hours ago. It ought to be an interesting experiment for everyone involved.''

''Ben—'' Her voice trembled. ''I'm afraid I've hurt you in a way you can't forgive. Please believe me when I tell you I wasn't attacking your dream. It's so fabulous, I still can't find the words.

''All I was trying to do is offer a few suggestions to

make it so perfect, people will clamor to live here. I'm so proud of what you've achieved. To be honest, I'm in awe of you.''

He raked a hand through his dark hair. "If that was awe, you've redefined the definition for all time.''

Her eyes glistened with tears. "Tell me I haven't ruined everything,'' she begged. "I couldn't bear it.''

"There's nothing to forgive, Terri. I knew what I was doing when I asked you to marry me. You've just reinforced it in an indelible way.''

She shook her head. "My father used to warn me I could get into trouble trying to fix everything for everybody.'' By now tears were dripping off her chin. She wiped them away. "This is one time I wish I'd taken his advice.''

Terri had no idea how Ben made it to the bedroom door ahead of her but he did. His hard-muscled frame barred the exit.

"Mrs. Herrick? We've just weathered our first storm. I have to tell you I found it more exciting than anything I've experienced in years.'' Before Terri could say a word, he cupped the side of her moist face with his free hand. "Don't ever change, or you wouldn't be you.''

In the next breath he pressed a tender kiss to her lips. It told her everything was going to be all right.

When he lifted his head, a moan of protest escaped her throat. He'd heard her. She couldn't recall it. But this was a time for honesty.

Looking up into his eyes she whispered, "As long as you still want me for your wife, I swear I'll do everything in my power to make you happy.''

"You already have.'' He put his arm around her shoulder. "Come on. Let's open our wedding presents. I know you're dying to. By the time we've finished, dinner will be here.''

She put an arm around his waist. Together they walked to the foyer. "When did you order it?"

"That's my secret. I told my favorite chef to surprise us."

Terri decided she was glad there'd been a rough moment. In getting so much emotion out of her system, she felt more natural and relaxed around him. Maybe it was good it had happened. He seemed in better spirits, too.

Though he might not be on fire for her, they had an inexplicable camaraderie that brought her inner contentment. That was one of the important ingredients missing in her marriage to Richard.

Ben helped her bring the gifts into the living room. They worked out a system. She took off wrappings and undid lids, then handed the gifts to Ben to actually open with his free hand. It didn't take long for the living room to look like a disaster area. At one point he was knee deep in paper and tissue. She ran for her camera and snapped some pictures.

They saved the family gifts until last. "Here's one from Parker." She handed it to him. "I think it's a picture."

"It's probably an eight-by-ten photograph of himself so you won't forget him. I guess I'd better read the card first. *This little filly's my favorite. She kind of reminds me of you.*"

Before Terri could avert her eyes, Ben held her gaze. "Want to tell me what that's all about?"

She smiled. "When he caught up with me in the hospital foyer, he said something about my running faster than a nervous filly being chased by a twister."

"There's nothing my little brother loves more than his horses. He's just paid you the supreme compliment." Ben lifted the framed photograph from the paper so she could see it, too.

"Oh, Ben! What a darling she is—I love it!"

"She's a little beauty all right. As long as we're on the subject, do you want to tell me why Parker gave Juanita Rosario money?"

CHAPTER EIGHT

TERRI would have answered his question, but just then the steward arrived from the kitchen with their wedding dinner.

Pears in champagne, tapas, spinach salad, stuffed shrimp, rack of lamb, yams in their jackets full of a buttery concoction of brown sugar and cinnamon followed by strawberry tarts laced with cordial and clotted cream.

Like happy children they ate in the middle of the mess and slowly opened the rest of their presents. Terri never wanted any of it to end.

Ben finished off the rest of the champagne in his goblet, then sat back on the couch. "I'll have to tell Andre he outdid himself."

"I want to meet him and thank him personally for this sumptuous feast. In fact I want to meet everyone who works on this ship. In time I hope to be able to call all of them by their first names."

His eyes played over her features. "That's an ambitious project, even for you."

"But not impossible."

"I doubt you've ever used that word."

She smiled. "I was just going to say the same thing about you. Otherwise there wouldn't be a floating city called the *Spirit of Atlantis,* and I wouldn't be married to its creator.

"Do you know I once had my fortune read by a Gypsy who told me I'd be carried off by a tall dark handsome stranger? When I asked her where he would take me, she got all excited and lifted her hands. 'You will go everywhere. You will see many sights.' Later I found out she told that to all my girlfriends.''

He chuckled.

"I felt kind of sorry for her. It's a hard way of life. Too bad I don't know her address. I could send her a postcard from the ship and tell her that her prediction came true. Of course I would explain that she left out the part about his looking like a mummy first.''

"I really frightened you, didn't I.''

"No. All I could think of was that you had to be suffering from claustrophobia. I felt like I needed your oxygen mask more than you did. Are you really okay now? I mean mentally, emotionally? If something like that had happened to me, I'd probably need counseling to get over it.''

"I *did* get therapy.''

"You mean the hospital provided it?''

"No. You did.''

She started to tremble. "I'm glad if I was able to help.''

"Everything you said and did brought me back to life. But none of it lasted long enough. That's why I came after you.''

"You've got me now. Creighton's ball and chain paperweight says it all.''

"That's a private joke.''

"You mean because even *you* didn't escape matrimony in the end?''

His lips twitched. "Something like that. Now where were we?''

Uh-oh. She scrambled to her feet and found a big plastic bag to start cleaning up the mess.

"Did the Rosario woman ask my brother for money?''

She paused. "No. He gave it to her out of the kindness of his heart.''

"Then I'll reimburse him.''

"Do you think—" Terri caught herself before she said the rest. A spurt of adrenaline helped her get back to the business of straightening the room. The last thing she wanted to do was create any friction, not after the lovely evening they'd spent together.

"Do I think what?"

She should have known Ben wouldn't let it go.

"Parker's photograph gave me the idea to do a collection of family pictures and memorabilia somewhere in the condo." In fact she'd just thought of something exciting for the master bedroom. "But we can talk about it another time."

He got up from the couch. "Before today, this was simply a place for me to eat and sleep. Now that I have a wife, I want us to turn it into our home. I'm looking forward to seeing your things arrive from Lead. In the meantime, do whatever your heart desires and I'll help."

"You spoil me." Her voice quivered.

"You're so unmercenary, it makes me want to. Now, finish telling me what you were going to say about Parker."

"That he'd probably be hurt if you tried to pay him back."

"And?" he persisted.

Warmth crept up her neck and into her face.

"You and Creighton have always watched out for him. I just think that this one time he probably enjoyed being the benefactor." Terri stared at her husband. "He adores you, but you'd be a hard act to follow."

She felt his eyes on her as she collected the gifts and put them in on the dining table. Tomorrow she would write out thank-you notes. When she came back in the living room, Ben had pushed the cart out of the way and was waiting for her.

"Along with all your exceptional attributes, nature also

gave you astounding insight into human nature. I'll leave it alone where Parker's concerned.''

Thank you. ''Since tomorrow's the last day before we sail, what can I do to help you?''

He rubbed the back of his neck absently. ''I have a checkup with Dr. Dominguez first thing in the morning. Afterward there's a little business to be taken care of at the downtown office. How would you like to go with me?''

''I'd love it. The people at the hospital took such wonderful care of you. I want to thank them in person.''

He looked pleased. ''Have you ever flown in a helicopter before?''

''Yes. Over Mount Rushmore.''

''Did you like it?''

''After I found my stomach.''

''I'm glad to hear it,'' he teased. ''If we fly, it will cut down on the time we have to be gone from the ship. This place is going to be a madhouse tomorrow with everyone arriving.''

''You must be so excited, I don't know how you're going to sleep!''

His eyes passed over her face and body in swift appraisal. ''Neither do I. How about a game of poker on my bed?''

Her heart thudded. He didn't want their evening to be over yet. ''What kind? Black Jack, or Spit In The Ocean?''

Ben shook his head. ''Where did you come from?''

She flashed him an innocent smile. ''There isn't much else to do on long blizzardy nights in the hills of South Dakota.''

After a pregnant silence he said, ''I think I've got a pack of cards in the top of my dresser. Let's go see, shall we?''

The receptionist looked at Terri expectantly. ''Can I get you a drink while you're waiting for your husband, Mrs. Herrick?''

Ben had just disappeared into his inner office in downtown Guayaquil. He'd told Terri he'd be a half hour at the most.

"No, thank you, but I was wondering if I could use one of the phones in here?"

The other woman's gaze flicked to an empty desk in the corner. "Maria hasn't come in to work yet. You can use hers."

"Does she have a phone directory?"

"In the bottom drawer."

"Thank you."

Terri hurried over to the desk in question and looked up the number of the Mirador Apartments. Juanita didn't have a phone, but the manager would have one. After some searching she found it and pressed the buttons. When a man answered she said, "Do you speak English?"

"A little."

"I would like to talk to Juanita Rosario. She lives in the apartment that belonged to Richard Jeppson."

"Ah. The Americano. He—how you say, *muerto.*"

"Yes. I know. I am Señora Jeppson. Is Juanita still living there?"

"Until tomorrow. Then she must leave."

"Could you tell her to come to the phone?"

"I no have time."

"I see. Thank you for your help, *señor.*"

Terri hung up the phone, afraid her sarcasm had been wasted on him.

Not to be defeated, she looked in her purse for another number and phoned Captain Ortiz. By some miracle he was there, but he sounded surprised to find out she was the person calling.

"Captain? I told Juanita Rosario she could get in touch

with me through you. Just now I tried to reach her at the apartment, but the manager wouldn't let me talk to her. Could I ask a great favor of you and get you to call him? Knowing you're the police, he'll probably agree.''

"I'd be happy to do that for you, but I must caution you that she's probably only trying to extort more money.''

"What if she were your daughter left all alone in the world? She's very young, and she's going to have a baby. The woman needs help. I was thinking of offering her a job.''

There was a drawn out silence. "You make a compelling case, *señora*. Give me the man's number.''

"Thank you, captain.'' After she'd complied she said, "If Juanita comes to the phone, tell her I would like her to call me on my cell phone.'' She gave him the number.

"I will do my best.''

"Thank you so much. You're a good man.''

"No, *señora. You* are a good woman. I envy your husband.'' With those kind words he rang off.

As she was hanging up, Ben came out the door of his office. Earlier at the hospital, the doctor had removed the dressings for good. No one except a few people who knew where to look would be able to tell he bore scars from his near-fatal accident.

Terri knew. His handsome face was all the more dear to her because of them.

His eyes looked around until he spied her at the desk. With the precision of a locked-on laser, he started toward her.

"Unlike most wives who would have taken advantage of the time to go shopping, mine is busy on the phone.''

She got up from the chair with a smile. "I was just taking care of a little, er, business.''

"Is that so.'' He pressed a kiss to her astonished mouth,

nodded to the receptionist, then swept Terri out of the room. The helicopter was waiting for them on the roof of the building.

During the flight back to the ship she gave Ben dozens of furtive glances while he patiently answered one call after another from his anxious co-workers. So many years of planning and preparation had gone into this incredible enterprise, she didn't know how he managed to stay calm and self-assured.

Anyone else would have been a nervous wreck. Not her husband. He was born for moments like this. In fact she knew he thrived on them.

How she loved him! Every day of life since she'd met him was more exciting than the last. More than once she found herself touching her lips that still tingled from the brief contact with his.

It had happened so naturally, she could have been forgiven for thinking he hadn't been able to help himself. But the receptionist's presence made fiction of her wishful thinking.

Everyone in the company knew about their marriage. It was important for him to personify the ardent honeymooner in public for a few more days at least.

Last night if people could have seen them playing one intense round of Black Jack after another until they'd resorted to cheating to win, no one would have believed it.

Or the fact that she'd finally dragged herself off to bed in the guest bedroom after his painkillers had knocked him out.

It was a good thing she hadn't had any expectations about her wedding night. But it still didn't prevent her from sobbing her heart out for what was left of it after they'd played their last poker hand.

Deep in thought, she hadn't realized how close they were to landing. Suddenly the helicopter dipped. She took one look out the window and cried her husband's name as the ship's heliport came up to meet them.

"It's a sight I never get tired of," he murmured.

At a height of twenty-three stories from the main deck, she could see the whole coast, the shipyard, the brilliant blue ocean, the pier bustling with a mass of humanity.

"It's so incredible, I can't believe anything's real." She turned to look at him. "To think you saw all this in your mind years ago. I'm married to my own Leonardo da Vinci."

"Hardly," he mocked. But as he continued to stare at her, his intelligent eyes gleamed with an inner light that penetrated to her soul. When the pilot told them they could deboard, she had no idea they'd touched down, or that the rotors had stopped whipping the air.

A few minutes later they were back in their condo foyer.

"Terri?" There was a certain quality in his voice she'd come to recognize.

She kept her eyes averted. "I know. You have to go. Don't worry about me. I have my own agenda."

"You think I'm not aware of that?" he teased.

"Phone me if you need me. I'll come running."

"I'll remember that." His voice grated.

Terri felt his hesitation before he stepped back inside the elevator. She held her breath until the door closed, separating her from the husband she loved more than she ever thought it possible to love a man. If he'd remained one more second, he would have been in no doubt how she felt about him.

Thankful there was so much work to do so she couldn't go to bed and sob her heart out a second time, she hurried into the dining room and got busy writing thank-you notes.

There were so many! Not only for the gifts from family and friends, but for the people like the captain of the ship, the organist, the chef and the stewards, the photographer, the dance band, all the staff who'd made their wedding day so exquisite.

When there was so much to do to get ready for the launching, it couldn't have been easy to plan a wedding at the last minute. In Terri's mind it revealed their profound respect and regard for her husband.

She still couldn't believe that of all the women he could have married, he'd chosen her. In her heart she prayed he would never regret it.

After working hard for the next couple of hours, she finished the last note, then separated them into piles to be mailed out or distributed to the staff. With that accomplished, she downed a peanut butter and jelly sandwich, grabbed her map of the *Atlantis* and took off for the post office in her sneakers.

In order to be of any help tomorrow, she decided to go exploring today so she'd know where to direct the new condo owners who might get lost on anything this gargantuan. One real plus to living on a ship this size—you could eat all you wanted because you ended up walking off the calories just to get from point A to point B.

Ben's private office, along with the other directors' offices, were all located on the twenty-third floor surrounding the board of directors' conference room. After she'd left the post office, she began her tour of discovery from the top floor, anxious to acquaint herself with Ben's inner sanctum.

It looked lived in. He'd obviously been working out of here for many months, but it needed plants and pictures. Perhaps the decorating firm hired for the project already had plans which hadn't been implemented yet. She'd find out from her husband.

The twenty-second floor to the fifth of the superstructure housed the condos. Floors one through four contained the shops, restaurants and businesses. She jogged around to get herself oriented.

So many thousands of details had to have been worked out on the drawing board first. Just estimating the number of lifeboats, preservers and provisions needed in case of an emergency boggled her mind. One day she'd like to shake the hand of the architects and engineers who'd brought Ben's dream to life.

The rest of the ship from the promenade deck down to the hull housed the crew and everything else necessary to the running of the massive vessel. On the flight to the city Ben had told her there was still space on A deck she could make into an office for the chamber of commerce. She headed there next, anxious to start planning her work space.

When she found it, she discovered a medium-size room with nothing in it, but it was ready for occupancy. That was perfect. Her belongings would be arriving before they set sail tomorrow. She would recreate the office she'd had at her apartment in South Dakota down to the pictures and momentos. It would make her feel right at home and wouldn't cost a dime!

Pleased beyond words, she kept touring the ship until she found the personnel office for the staff. There was a sign in front of the thirtyish looking blond man seated at the desk. John Reagan, Manager.

"Mr. Reagan?"

He looked up from the computer. After an admiring male glance he got to his feet. "Hello."

"Hi. I'm Terri Herrick."

The revelation seemed to take him back for a moment, but he recovered just as quickly. "How do you do, Mrs. Herrick. We all heard he got married yesterday. Lucky man," he said under his breath but she heard him.

"I'm the lucky one." They shook hands.

He grinned. "Are you lost by any chance?"

"Not yet, but the day isn't over yet. I came to talk to you."

"Sure. Please. Sit down."

"Thank you." She perched on one of the chairs. "You and I will be neighbors. I'm the new head of the chamber of commerce a few doors down."

"You're kidding. I didn't even know there was one on the ship."

"It's just been announced. Anyway, I'll explain the reason for my visit. There might be a young pregnant woman coming aboard who's hit hard times and needs a job. I'm not sure how much English she speaks. Until I know more about her, I have no idea what her qualifications are.

"She's going to have her baby within the week, so in any event she wouldn't be able to work until she's back on her feet. I already know the rule about no babies, but that might change in the future.

"My question is this—are there any rooms still vacant for a potential staff member?"

"Quite a few."

"Are there any singles?"

"Some."

"If she could stay in one of them until she goes into labor, I'll pay for her room and board. One of the restaurants can send her meals. It may be that after she's released from the hospital, she won't be able to work on board and will have to be flown back to Guayaquil, but I'll worry about that later."

"Sure. I don't have a problem with that."

"Please don't say yes because I'm married to Mr. Herrick."

"If we needed the space, I'd have to tell you no. But so far, so good. Seeing as she's about to have a baby and won't need the room very long, it's fine with me."

"Thank you, Mr. Reagan."

"John."

"Thanks, John. The thing is, I don't know if she'll even show up, but I thought I'd better check with you ahead of time just in case."

"No problem."

"Wonderful. Now could you do one more thing for me? I need you to write down what I'm going to say to her in Spanish so I'll be able to communicate with her if she calls me first. Do you mind?"

"Not at all."

In a few minutes she felt prepared. "Thanks. I'll see you again soon."

She left the room on a run and headed for the supermarket on the first floor. No matter the hour, she wanted a homemade dinner waiting for Ben when he came in. Meat loaf, baked potatoes, fresh shelled peas and fruit salad were easy. An hour later she'd set the round table in the dinette area. Everything was ready.

"Terri?"

At the sound of his familiar male voice, her heart turned over. "In the kitchen!" she called out as she took the food from the oven.

There were footsteps. "Hmm. Something smells good. I didn't expect *this*."

She wheeled around to face him. "I hope you've got time to eat before you have to put out another fire."

His eyes searched hers. "I'll make time. I'm starving."

"Sit down and I'll serve you."

Within minutes he was practically wolfing down his dinner. She'd made enough meat loaf for leftovers, but it had all disappeared by the time they'd finished their meal.

He finally looked up at her a little sheepishly. "I was even hungrier than I thought."

Terri couldn't help smiling. "It tells me you've had a

very busy day, and it's not over yet. Go on. Whenever you come home, I'll have another video waiting which is guaranteed to put you to sleep. You need one for your big day tomorrow.''

"What movie is that?''

"Attack of the Killer Tomatoes.''

"The *what?*'' He broke into laughter. "I'm afraid I've never heard of it.''

"It's everyone's favorite in South Dakota.''

He reached for her hand across the table and squeezed it. "I can't wait.'' After letting her go, he got up from the table. "The dinner was fabulous.''

"Thank you.''

"What are you going to do now?''

"This and that.''

He paused in the entry. "I'll hurry.''

Terri cleared the table and did the dishes, aware she was *too* happy. In a state hovering dangerously close to euphoria, her cell phone rang. The caller ID said out of area. Was it Juanita? She clicked on.

"This is Mrs. Herrick.''

"Señora? It's Captain Ortiz.''

"Yes, Captain?''

"I have Juanita Rosario with me.''

She blinked. "Where are you?''

"We're in my police car at the pier next to the second floating dock. After you and I spoke, I phoned the manager. He acted very strange so I drove out there. It seems he wouldn't let her stay another day unless she paid him all the back rent your ex-husband owed.

"She handed over the money you gave her, then he told her to leave. Now she has nothing. But she swears the manager was lying. I believe her. Therefore, I had some officers take him to the station for questioning. I told her what you were prepared to do for her. She came willingly, but I fear she's ill.''

''Do you think the baby's coming?''

''I don't know.''

''Thank you for going beyond the call of duty, captain. I'll think of a way to repay you. If you'll keep her there, I'll call the hospital and ask them to send a medical team ashore to bring her aboard. Tell her I'll be waiting in the E.R.''

For the next hour she was on pins and needles as she paced the E.R. lounge watching for the EMTs to bring in Juanita. Terri had already given what information she could to the triage nurse. When asked about insurance, Terri said she'd be personally responsible for the bill.

By the time this was over, she would have used up her savings, but it didn't matter. Not when compared to the worth of two lives which were in danger.

At ten to ten, Ben left Carlos checking on some minor things and headed for the condo. Since dinner, getting back to Terri was all he could think about. The second the private elevator door allowed him entry, he called her name.

The fact that she didn't answer back didn't mean she wasn't here. He went to the kitchen first in search of her. Everything looked tidy, the dishes were done. She'd cleared away all the gifts from the dining room table. Maybe she'd gone to bed.

He walked through the condo to the guest bedroom. Her bed was still made up. With pounding heart he hurried to his bedroom in the hope he'd find her asleep on his bed in front of the TV waiting for him.

When she was nowhere to be found, his disappointment was greater than he could believe. It hit him then just how profoundly Terri had affected his life. Until the accident which had brought her into his world, he'd never felt anything missing from his bachelor routine.

For years he'd come and gone from his apartment in Guayaquil, and then more recently from the condo, without giving it a thought. When he did spend time with a woman, it was usually someone he'd met at a party when he'd flown to the States or Europe on business.

Then suddenly when he was at his lowest ebb in that hospital room, an angelic looking face appeared above him. A pair of eyes peered into his with so much pathos, it changed the meaning of existence for him.

Where was she?

He pulled out his cell phone and rang her. By the time she finally answered, he had to tamp down hard on his emotions to act normal. She had every right to go where she wanted and do whatever she felt like.

Ben had no business being upset because she wasn't home waiting for him like a dutiful little wife. She'd already tried to do that for her ex-husband with disastrous results.

Do you honestly think she would put herself through that again for you, Herrick?

"Hi. Thought I'd check in with you."

"H-how is everything going so far?"

His fingers tightened around the phone. Everything had been going fine until now. "Good."

"Where are you?"

Something was definitely wrong.

"Home."

"Oh—I didn't realize you'd get through your work so fast."

So fast? It was after ten. He sucked in his breath. "How much longer do you think you'll be?"

"I—I'm not sure."

She was being so evasive, it scared the hell out of him.

His brows knit together. "Do you want me to come where you are?"

"No— I mean—now that you're at the condo, you need to get to sleep. I'll be home when I can."

"What's wrong?" He'd had all he could take.

"I'll explain later."

"Where are you, Terri?"

Her eyes closed tightly. She'd alarmed her husband when it was absolutely the last thing she'd wanted to do.

It had been her intention to tell him about Juanita. Just not tonight, not on the eve of the embarkment he'd been looking forward to for years!

He had the weight of the world on his shoulders right now. To worry him about anything else was killing her, but there was no help for it. When a baby decided to enter the world, it didn't check to see if it was convenient.

"I'm at the hospital w—"

"Lord—"

"Ben— I'm all right!" she cried, but the line had gone dead.

Oh, no.

Knowing she could expect her husband to arrive any minute, she left the waiting room and went out in the hall to the elevator. While she watched for him, she reproached herself over and over again for keeping silent about Juanita.

After the wedding, she should have told Ben what Captain Ortiz had said to her in the wedding line—that Juanita had been trying to get in touch with her because she was in trouble.

This was yet another example of Terri trying to keep problems away from her husband and fix one for someone else at the same time. Only it had backfired in a way she was afraid he wouldn't be able to forgive.

She heard the ping of the elevator. "Ben!" she cried as her husband emerged with an anxiety-ridden face.

He took one look at her and suddenly she was in his arms, sling and all. "Thank God." His voice sounded so shaken, it was a revelation to her.

"You hung up before I could tell you I wasn't the patient," she whispered into his neck.

Afraid she might lose control and pull his head down so she could kiss him, she backed out of his arms. Maybe it was her imagination, but he seemed reluctant to let her go.

She noticed his chest rise and fall sharply, as if he were trying to catch his breath. "What happened?"

"It's a long story, but I'd rather tell you about it when we're back in the condo."

"Who was hurt?"

Terri moistened her lips nervously. "It's Juanita Rosario."

His expression underwent another alteration. She saw that his eyes had darkened. "What's she doing on the *Atlantis?*"

"Having a caesarian section."

He blinked.

"A little while ago the obstetrician told me the baby was in trouble, so he made the decision to operate. I was waiting to hear if everything had gone all right before I went back upstairs. Then you called."

She could hear his brilliant mind working, turning things over until he'd made sense of it.

"Parker made a big mistake when he gave her money."

"No—" She shook her head. "It doesn't have anything to d—"

"Mrs. Herrick?" At the sound of the triage nurse's voice, Terri swung around.

The other woman had popped her head outside the E.R.

doors. "Oh— Mr. Herrick! What an honor! Congratulations on your marriage!"

"Thank you," he muttered.

"Mrs. Herrick? Dr. Cardenas wants to talk to you now. Just so you won't worry, the patient gave birth to a beautiful little five-pound daughter. Just think—the first baby born on the *Atlantis*! The staff couldn't be more delighted. What an amazing night this has turned out to be!"

Ben's arm tightened around Terri's waist as they walked toward the excited nurse. "That woman took the words right out of my mouth."

CHAPTER NINE

"BEN? May I come in?"

"The door is open."

It had only taken her a minute to slip on her nightgown and robe, but she'd given him a little longer to get ready for bed.

She walked all the way in the room. It was dark except for the light coming from the hallway. "I have your pills."

He'd already slid under the covers and lay on his back. "I took some in the bathroom."

Terri set the water glass on the table.

This time he didn't pat her side of the bed. She sat down anyway.

"I'm going to tell you everything from the beginning so you'll understand."

Without stopping for breath, Terri launched into a full explanation of her visits to the apartment where she gave Juanita money. She told him how she'd used Captain Ortiz and Parker to help translate for her. When Parker added his contribution, it was a spontaneous gesture meant to back up Terri.

Ben didn't break in, so she sped on with her account of the conversation with John Reagan in personnel, and the subsequent phone call from Captain Ortiz at the pier.

"I swear I never intended to use a dime of your money for this. Before we left Lead, I withdrew all my savings. It's not a lot, but there's enough to pay her hospital bill and board until she gets back on her feet."

"Which won't be for some time considering she had to undergo a caesarean," he said in a surprisingly calm voice.

"I'm afraid she can't stay in staff quarters with a newborn."

"I know."

"So what were you thinking?"

Grateful he didn't sound angry she said, "I hoped the hospital would let her stay long enough to get back on her feet. Then I'd fly to Guayaquil with her and help her find work and a place to live with her baby."

"That's very commendable. Now let's hear Plan B."

Her face went hot. "Well— I guess if I could make a case with the board for allowing families with children to live on the ship, maybe one of the condos that hasn't sold could be turned into a day care center."

At this point Ben made a strange sound in his throat, much like the kind she'd heard coming from him when he was mummified.

"It would give the mothers a break for a few hours or all day. I realize we'd have to get a trained, licensed person to head the center." She spoke faster and faster.

"Possibly they could train Juanita so she could be licensed, too. The two of them could live in one part of the condo with her baby, and set up the center in the other.

"If down the road Juanita wanted to leave the ship, she'd have a skill so she could find a good job elsewhere."

He sat up and leaned toward her. "And when all these babies are too old for the nursery, then what?" he drawled.

"It would mean there would have to be a preschool, and an elementary and middle school. The thing is, while I was getting acquainted with the ship this afternoon, I noticed that on the Sun Deck there's a whole area in the aft section that hasn't been designated for anything specific yet.

"If the schools were put there, they'd be near pools and outdoor activities that would be perfect for recess."

He reached out to brush some blond tendrils away from

her cheek. His touch sent a shock wave through her body. "I'm afraid the directors have a casino in mind."

"Casino— But there are several dozen bars on the ship. Surely some of them could be turned into *dens of iniquity* at much less expense."

She felt his body shake. He was laughing at her again. At least his mood had improved since they'd left the hospital.

"I can tell there's a lot more on your mind. I'm willing to listen, but I can almost hear your teeth chattering. Get under the covers and make yourself comfortable."

Her heart almost went into fibrillation. He'd just asked her to get in bed with him. She'd been wanting to do just that ever since she'd met him.

Was he testing the waters? Or was it a case of his being too tired to sit up talking to her any longer?

He was a man who liked to do the chasing.

He *had* asked...

Desperate to find out, she stood up and pulled the covers back so she could get in.

"I'm sure that feels better," he murmured as she pulled the covers to her chin.

He was only a few feet away from her. She could feel all that male warmth. Terri would sell her soul to be wrapped up in it.

"What is it about men that they love to sleep in freezing cold rooms?"

"I didn't realize you'd done a study on the subject."

"I haven't exactly. But my dad and Richard were the same way. Beth says Tom's so bad, he runs the air-conditioning when it's sixty degrees out."

His legs stirred. "Maybe it's a macho thing. One of those mysteries of the male psyche not meant to be understood."

"I can't explain PMS either, so I guess that evens the score."

The bed shook. "Is this your way of telling me you're having a bad day?"

"No." She chuckled. "It was just a comment since we were talking about mysteries."

"How about solving one for me?"

There was something in his tone that sounded serious.

"If I can."

"I understand your need to help Juanita. But to go as far as to try and help her find a job—"

"You probably think it's weird."

"No. But I have wondered if it means you haven't let go of Richard yet."

"Richard?" she cried in exasperation. "He has nothing to do with it!" she declared with every fiber of her being. "Our marriage was over on the honeymoon. But I'd made vows and was determined to keep them. I thought, if I could have a child, then I could pour out my love on it.

"As I explained before, Richard happened to be away both times I lost my babies. But what I didn't tell you was that I found out he'd made several women pregnant while he was in California. That's why he moved around, so he wouldn't have to take responsibility."

She felt him reach for her hand and cling to it.

"Ben—when you told me Richard had only worked down here for four months, I realized Juanita's baby couldn't be his. That meant the birth father had abandoned her, just the way Richard had abandoned me and those two other women."

Tears sprang to her eyes unbidden. "Captain Ortiz finally told me her story. She ran away from an abusive home, was abused by the man who got her pregnant. Though she knew that Richard was seeing other women, that he partied with them, she stayed with him because at least he didn't slap her around.

"It made me so sick for all the women who love bad men and don't have the tools to get out." She half sobbed the words.

"After you told me Richard had drowned, I thought 'oh no,' she's been abandoned again. The cycle's never going to stop. She'll go on being abused for the rest of her life. The same thing will probably happen to her child.

"You should see her, Ben. She's young and beautiful, but she'll go to her death never knowing the good life.

"It made me so angry, I can't tell you. Captain Ortiz made me angry at first. He said, 'Don't give her money. She'll be back for more.'

"The point is, she didn't ask me for anything. I had to throw it at her. She almost didn't take it from Parker. I kept thinking, there but for the grace of God go I. My parents raised me in a loving home. I never knew emotional abuse until I lived with Richard. Fortunately I had an education, a job, backing.

"Juanita has none of that. Captain Ortiz must have sensed her plight because he finally softened enough to tell me she'd been trying to get in touch with me for help. He didn't have to tell me that. He could have left it alone, and I'd have been none the wiser. But his conscience won out.

"So here we are. Stuck on your dream ship with my problem. One you didn't ask for, and didn't need. You were better off when you didn't have a wife. I had no right to tell you what improvements I thought should be made.

"I'm sorry, Ben. So sorry."

Pulling her hand away, she jumped out of bed and started running.

"Terri? For the love of heaven, come back here."

Afraid he might follow her into her bedroom, she dashed into her bathroom and locked the door.

Sure enough, she saw the handle turn. "Terri, we have to talk. Open the door."

"Please go away. I promise that as soon as Juanita can get on an airplane, I'll leave with her and you'll never have to deal with a liability like me again."

"That's your PMS talking. Go ahead and have a good cry. By the time you come back to bed I'll have the room at a toasty seventy degrees. How does that sound?"

"Ben—tomorrow's the biggest day of your life. You need your sleep."

"I need something else a lot more. Be my wonderful wife and come and give me a leg massage. It worked like magic before. I could use a little of that tonight. Even a business titan like me is a bit shaky right now thinking about what's going to happen in the morning."

She sniffed. "You're really nervous?"

"What if after all this, it doesn't sail?"

"That's the most preposterous thing I've ever heard."

"That's why I need you. To tell me everything's going to be all right."

Her husband was such a tower of strength to the people around him, it never occurred to anyone he had normal human fears. But Terri had seen his human side the first time she'd looked into those unforgettable gray eyes filled with pain and pleading.

Without conscious thought she reached for her lotion and unlocked the door. Her heart sank because he was no longer there.

No doubt he'd gone back to bed. He probably assumed she'd stay in the bathroom until she thought it was safe to come out. But that would be immature and selfish of her.

"Why don't you turn on your stomach and I'll do the backs of your legs first," she said after she'd ventured into his room once more.

He tossed the covers aside and rolled over. She pushed

his pajama legs to the knee, then got started. At one point she sat down so she could do both legs at once. Loving him as much as she did, it was ecstasy to be able to worship him with her hands.

"That feels like heaven. Don't ever stop."

She kept up the rhythm until she heard the deep, even sounds of his breathing. Very carefully she put the covers over him. He'd fallen asleep.

Terri knew he needed it badly. Her husband would have to be up and ready to go by six-thirty for a day that would go down in history, starting with the ship's christening.

Ben explained that Captain Rogers' wife would have that honor. Once she'd broken the champagne bottle against the hull of the *Atlantis*, their voyage would begin around the tip of South America.

Fifteen hours later Terri stood alone against the railing on the promenade deck with the stiff breeze blowing her tangerine-colored suit skirt against her legs. The shipyard and pier had long since faded from view.

Ben had arranged for both their families to ride in one of the many tugboats that followed the *Atlantis* for a distance. As Ben had stood behind her, he'd put his binoculars in her hands. She'd been able to find their boat and see their faces.

Together they'd taken turns watching and waving until all the boats became mere specks on the horizon. The whole time Ben had wrapped his free arm around her neck while they'd stood locked against the railing. She'd felt cocooned in the warmth of his hard body and legs. Several times he'd buried his face in her hair.

Emotions had to have been running rampant inside him. Joy, excitement, relief that everything was going perfectly. Terri was so thankful that he was alive to see this day come, she hadn't been able to stop the tears from falling.

"You can see your family whenever you want," he'd

whispered against her ear. For once he hadn't been able to divine her thoughts, but she was glad for that. Better to let him go on believing it was a wrench to leave her loved ones. He still didn't know *he* had become her whole world.

The ship was in open sea now.

Terri had taken two different ferries with her family when they'd visited the Puget Sound area of Washington on vacation, but she'd never experienced being on an ocean going vessel before. The motion of the ship would take some getting used to, however she didn't feel queasy or anything.

Before Ben had left her side to join Carlos and the chief engineer for an inspection now that they were underway, he'd urged her to take some seasickness tablets, just in case. To humor him, she said she'd try one as soon as she returned to their condo. He'd pressed a kiss to her neck before walking away.

But that was several hours ago, and she was still in their same spot near the bow with other condo residents, watching the ocean in rapt wonder, trying to take it all in. A blimp from one of the major television networks filming the unprecedented event was still following their progress.

With the sky overcast, the water appeared a grayer blue today. According to Ben, they were headed into bad weather. He was looking forward to it, anxious to see how the *Atlantis* handled before they reached Buenos Aires on the Atlantic side of the great South American continent. There they would take on more condo owners.

When her stomach growled, she left her vigil and went back to the condo for a sandwich and a change into casual clothes and sneakers. Then she headed for the hospital, eager to see Juanita's baby.

En route she received a call from the cargo hold. Where did she want her belongings taken?

It shouldn't have surprised her business was going on

as usual, even on their first day at sea. That meant her plan to visit the nursery would have to be put off for a while.

She told them she'd be right there and headed in the direction of the hold. Of course being right there took a little time on a ship four thousand feet long.

Beth, bless her heart, had organized the packing. She'd labeled the boxes, kitchen, study, living room, bedroom, bathroom. That made it easy. Everything was to go to the condo except the boxes marked study. Terri accompanied the latter to her new place of business and sent the rest upstairs.

Once she got started opening everything, she lost track of time. John Reagan saw what was going on and came in to help her set up her desk and computer. She felt guilty about taking him away from his work and told him she could do everything just fine.

"Hey— I put a sign on the door that if anyone needed me, just look inside here. So far no one has come, so show me what you want done next."

"Well—that big crate has my love seat in it."

"Let me run back for my tool kit."

He returned in a flash. While they worked he asked her about Juanita. When Terri told him what had happened he said, "Have you seen the baby yet?"

"No. But I will after I'm through here."

He laughed. "What a wake-up call for the hospital!"

Terri could still see the shock on her husband's face when he'd found out. "I'm sure it was…" Her voice trailed.

"Okay—what shall I do next?"

"Help me decide where to hang these." She'd pulled out four poster-size framed photographs of the various tourist attractions in and around the Black Hills. She handed him the top one to hang over her desk.

"Hey, I've been to Mount Rushmore. It's amazing."

"It is."

"A couple of my buddies visited it while we were in Sturges for the motorcycle confab."

She flicked him a surprised glance. "You ride a Harley?"

"Yes, ma'am. I've got it on board. Whenever we get shore leave, I plan to ride it around."

"Then you're going to like *this*." The next picture was a well-known photograph of motorcycle riders in their sunglasses, head scarves and leathers driving through Sturges. One of the Hell's Angels had autographed it for her.

John went crazy over it. She knew enough about guys who were into cycles to know they had an intense love affair with their bikes.

"I once had a boyfriend who owned a Harley," she confessed. "My parents never knew he let me take it for rides. There was this old track nobody used. I got good enough on it that I was thinking of buying one myself. He used to call me his Mama!"

"Yeah?" His eyes blazed with new interest. He finished tapping a nail into the wall over the love seat so he could hang it. When he was through, he stepped back, admiring it with satisfaction.

Then he looked at her. "Maybe you'd like to ride on the back of mine? I could take you places you'd never get to see by car."

"That's an interesting offer," came a deep male voice from behind them.

They both whipped around at the same time.

"Ben—"

Her heart pounded with excitement every time her husband came near. In his ship whites, his looks were so appealing, there wasn't a man anywhere to compare to him.

Unfortunately his expression revealed no emotion at all.

He just stood there staring at the two of them through shuttered lids.

"Mr. Herrick," John greeted him. "Congratulations on your marriage."

"Thank you, Mr. Reagan."

The negative tension coming from her husband made Terri uneasy. "John was kind enough to help me unpack and get situated."

"It looks like he beat me to it."

The younger man smiled. "I didn't have anything else to do. May I say it's a pleasure to have your wife on board."

"I dare say you've seen more of my bride than I have."

Uh-oh. If Terri didn't know better, she would think her husband was jealous. But he couldn't be!

Ben's piercing gaze flicked to hers. "Since there's nothing more to be done here, shall we check on the new baby before dinner, or did you both do that already?

"No," she said in a quiet voice. He *was* angry.

John must have sensed it because he looked at his watch. "I had no idea of the time. I'll see you tomorrow, Mrs. Herrick."

"Don't forget your toolbox."

"I almost forgot." He put his things away and shut it. "Thanks." As he passed her husband, he nodded to him before disappearing out the door.

Ben stood there like a piece of impenetrable wood.

"What do you think?" she asked in the brightest voice she could muster.

"We have an office supplier on board who would have outfitted your new business to your specifications. I had no idea you intended to put your personal things in here."

Why was he so upset?

"The condo wasn't built with a study," she explained. "Since all this was in mine at home, I thought I could save you a little money by placing my own things around in here. If they look too shabby or don't convey the right image, we can have everything taken upstairs.''

''I'm not bordering on bankruptcy yet, but I appreciate your concern for our household finances. As for this office, you've created a haven of charm that expresses your personality. When the Garden Shop finishes decorating the top floor, I'll tell them to talk to you about the kind of plants you'd like in here. Shall we go?''

Terri left with him, determined to get back in his good graces if it killed her. ''Your worries were for naught,'' she teased playfully as they headed for the hospital.

He made no comment, but that didn't daunt her.

''Your dream ship has been sailing the high seas all day and hasn't broken down once.''

She heard his sharp intake of breath. ''That's what they said about the *Titanic*.''

Terri burst into laughter and grasped his hand. To her joy his fingers tightened around hers. ''That's one movie we won't ever watch. Yesterday I bought frozen pizza which I like to doctor up a certain way. What do you say we watch the *Killer Tomatoes* in bed and stuff ourselves.''

''You're not seasick?'' He pushed open the doors leading into the hospital.

''Not yet.''

''I'm surprised the pills didn't make you sleepy.''

''I didn't need them. Do you know it never occurred to me until right this second how terrible it would be if I were the kind who got deathly sick on the water? After all the trouble I've caused you, and then that, too…''

''Good evening, Mr. and Mrs. Herrick,'' a female voice broke in before her husband had a chance to respond. It was the same triage nurse from before. She beamed at them.

''I wondered when we'd see the two of you in here.

Heaven knows, everybody else on the ship has already been by to look at the baby through the nursery window.''

''How's the mother?'' Ben asked before Terri could.

''She's been in a lot of pain and is sedated right now, but you're welcome to peek at her little girl. I'll call for one of the nurses to show you where to go.''

In a few minutes they were standing before the glass while another nurse wearing a mask in the newborn unit held up Juanita's tiny baby for their inspection.

''Oh Ben—'' Terri cried. ''Isn't she precious— Look at all that dark curly hair. Juanita's so lucky. I hope when she's feeling better, she'll let me hold the baby.''

He let go of her hand and put his arm around her shoulders. ''I have no doubt of it. In the meantime your husband is salivating for that pizza you were talking about.''

By some miracle he didn't sound upset anymore. Counting her blessings she said, ''I'm hungry, too. Let's go.''

So far Ben's bed was her favorite place on earth. They ate, drank and played cards on it while they laughed at the absurd film. He made her promise to wait until the following evening when he would help her open all the other boxes from Lead spread around in the foyer and living room.

Halfway through a rousing game of Spit in the Ocean, she recalled something he'd said to her in the driveway of her mother's house.

My interest in seeing your apartment stems from pure interest in getting to know you better. Suddenly she thought she understood what had gone on inside her husband.

''Ben— I'm sorry I didn't wait for you to help me set up my office. I would have been pained if our positions had been reversed and I'd walked in on you sharing something from your past with a virtual stranger.

''I was just trying to get things done and out of the way

so I could be of help to you. I didn't stop to think how it would affect you. It's probably too late to promise that I'll never knowingly do anything that thoughtless again.''

"You owe me no apology, Terri. If I came off sounding surly, it's because I couldn't find you in the condo. Frankly I was disappointed because I had to look for you. It was a purely selfish reaction on my part.''

Don't ever get over it, her heart cried.

"Ben, there's something else.''

"What is it?''

"I've been feeling the fool ever since I told all your colleagues that I was going to be the new head of the chamber of commerce. It was a perfectly ridiculous thing to say.

"The thing is, I don't know how to be a secretary to anyone, let alone to someone like you. I feared I could never measure up, but I wanted you to be proud of me. So I clung to the only thing I knew how to do. However it isn't what you need.

"What I'm trying to say is, if you'll be patient with me, I'll try to be a good secretary to you. But you'll have to show me how.''

She started cleaning up the mess they'd made on the bed. "There's no sign on the door of my new office yet. Let's just leave it that way. I'll report there for work every weekday morning.

"You can buzz me from your office and tell me what you'd like me to do. I'll try to do it. In time, maybe I'll get to the point where I'll be able to function somewhat on my own.''

He picked up what she couldn't carry and followed her to the kitchen.

"Let's not make any snap decisions tonight. After breakfast in the morning when we're both fresh, why don't you come to my office with me and we'll talk about everything."

"I'll be happy to." She finished wiping off the counters. "You sound tired. How's the pain in your shoulder?"

"It's fine. I won't need to take any pills tonight."

"That's because you've been wearing your sling."

"With you around to remind me, I have no choice."

"No. You *don't*."

She finally dared to look at him. "I haven't told you what a remarkable speech you made today at the launching. You held everyone spellbound. In remembrance of it, I had a little gift made for you in Lead."

Her mother had brought it with her. "It's in my bedroom. I'll be right back." She dashed through the condo to get it, then returned to the kitchen. "Here."

To some degree he was able to use the fingers of his other hand to help undo the paper. He lifted the lid.

It was a man's gold ring with a black onyx face. The word *Atlantis* and today's date had been artistically hammered into it with Black Hills gold. "I think the artisan did a lovely job considering the time constraints."

There was a long period of silence. "Will you put it on for me?" he finally said in a thick-sounding voice.

She slid it on to the ring finger of his right hand. Before she could pull her hand away, he grasped it and brought it to his lips. "You've given me a wedding ring, and now *this*. Two treasures I'll cherish forever."

Her disappointment that he didn't try to kiss her on the mouth devastated her. The opportunity had been there, but he'd chosen not to take advantage of it. When was she going to learn that you couldn't force desire? It had to come from Ben of its own accord.

Averting her eyes, she eased away from him. It was time to get out of there before she fell apart.

"I don't know about you, but the motion of the ship

has made me sleepy. Good night, Ben. See you in the morning.''

She disappeared to her room. As soon as she could shut the door, she threw herself on the bed and buried her face in the pillow. It was sopping wet by the time oblivion took over.

When morning came, she was aware of the ship's motion more strongly than the day before. They'd come into rougher seas. She sat up and peered out the window. It didn't look that much different from yesterday, but there was definitely more wind.

One glance at her watch and she groaned. Ten after nine. She'd slept through her alarm. Why hadn't Ben wakened her? She'd planned to get their breakfast.

What a great wife she was turning out to be!

She washed her hair and showered in record time. It didn't take long to blow-dry it and put on lipstick. Then she donned a pair of tailored white pants and matching top over which she wore a navy blue cotton blazer.

After slipping into a pair of comfortable white cork wedgies, she dashed into the kitchen for a bite to eat before she reported to Ben's office. To her surprise she found a note on the fridge.

Your breakfast is in the oven, sleepyhead. After so many gifts, it was the least I could do to show my appreciation. Come upstairs whenever you're ready. Ben.

She quickly opened the oven door. He'd left a plate of sausage, scrambled eggs and cinnamon toast warming.

Ben— It was such a sweet thing to do.

Where he was concerned, she seemed to plumb a never ending well of tears. She fought to keep them from falling, but it was a losing battle.

Everything tasted delicious. She ate all of it and finished with a glass of orange juice. One more trip to the bathroom to brush her teeth and wipe her eyes. Now she felt ready to put on a bright face to hide her heartache from the husband she adored.

Their private elevator took her straight to the lobby opposite the board of directors' conference room. She could hear voices. It sounded like they were in a meeting.

Ben had told her to come upstairs, but he'd probably assumed she would show up before this. Afraid to disturb, she walked around to his private office and peeked inside the door.

"Come all the way in."

Her husband had spotted her. Now he was on his feet behind his large oak desk looking very much like the CEO in a pale blue silk suit. She felt his scrutiny as she made her way over to him.

"I'm so sorry I'm late," she began.

"Don't apologize. You needed your sleep."

"Thank you for the delicious breakfast. I loved it."

"Good. It's about time I did something considerate for my wife for a change."

Her stunned blue gaze flew to his. "What are you talking about?" she cried. "I'm so spoiled now, it's pathetic. You've treated me like a princess from the moment we met. It's time I started my training. What would you like me to do first?"

His gaze had narrowed on her mouth, distracting her. "Come with me." He walked around his desk and grasped her hand. When she realized where he was headed, she pulled back.

"If you want me to take notes of your meeting, I don't know shorthand."

"You have a very antiquated idea of what a secretary does these days. We already have a device that records everything and prints it."

"Then I don't understand why you want me to go in there."

"Because I'm asking you," he stated quietly. "Is that a good enough reason?"

His question made chaos of her emotions, but she had said she would try to be a good secretary. "Yes. Of course."

"I'm glad that's settled."

He shifted his hand to her shoulder and ushered her into the boardroom. A sea of faces she recognized from the reception turned to look at her. One by one they smiled and nodded as Ben led her to the head of the table.

"Gentlemen? You've all met my new bride, Terri. If you recall at our reception, she gave a speech in which she alluded to some oversights having to do with the *Atlantis*.

"This morning I've asked her in her capacity as the head of our new chamber of commerce to give us her perspective on several issues she deems of vital importance."

He gave her shoulder a squeeze. "Take all the time you need."

CHAPTER TEN

RARELY in her life had Terri been at a loss for words.

Thirty billionaires of every nationality who were the brains of megacorporations sat there politely waiting for her to speak.

When she'd found certain items lacking in the brochure and had voiced her opinion, she never realized just how deeply she'd hurt Ben. She assumed this was his way of letting her know she'd scarred him.

What better method of retribution than to throw her into the deep end among his colleagues, then sit by and watch her try to save herself.

How horrible last night must have been for him. Under the circumstances it would have taken every bit of will-power to tolerate kissing her hand. To think she'd been waiting for him to crush her mouth in long suppressed passion.

A shudder racked her body.

There was only one thing to do. She would have to present her case in the most professional way possible. The last thing she would ever want to do is embarrass him.

But when she walked out of here, she would pack the few things she needed and arrange a flight to take her from the ship to the nearest airport on the mainland. From there she'd make arrangements to get home to Lead.

Ben was in too deep to divorce her, so she would do him the favor of leaving. No one had to know what was going on. At least not for a while. He could tell people she was seasick, or that her mother was ill.

Unfortunately the situation with Juanita was something

he would have to take care of. The poor thing couldn't be moved yet, and Terri couldn't stay. If there was one thing to be thankful for, she hadn't unpacked anything in the condo. Ben could send it all back where it came from.

"Good morning, gentlemen. I didn't realize my husband would ask me to talk to you about something we discussed in private. That's what comes from a whirlwind marriage."

Everyone laughed.

"I can only liken this occasion to that moment when the president of the United States first takes possession of the White House. There's a thirty-day honeymoon period where certain sins are forgiven. I hope you will extend me that same grace."

To her relief they were still smiling. The only person whose face wasn't visible was her husband's. Because of that, she could go on.

"As you can imagine, we had so many other things on our minds, I never saw the brochure of Ben's dream ship, as I like to call it, until a few days ago. Because I'm a new wife, my thoughts have been centered on raising a family, maybe having a dog to love.

"But I soon learned about the covenants that have been drawn up concerning the sale of the condos, for instance the no pets policy, and the restriction on children below high school age.

"When I realized this was a floating city that wasn't interested in having babies and animals aboard, I guess I felt depressed. It was an emotional reaction on my part. But to me a true community is a cross section of life.

"What I told my husband was that if he and I were a couple in the market for a condo on anything as fabulous as the *Atlantis,* I'm afraid I wouldn't have considered it after finding out about the restrictions.

"I understand the reasons for them. It's obvious you didn't have couples like us in mind. But it's my opinion that you'd have every condo sold in a few days if you lifted those restrictions.

"Having said that, I beg you to remember one thing— if I'd known what Ben had in mind before he brought me in here, I would have told him I revered all of you too much to risk offending you."

Without looking at Ben she put her hand on his shoulder and squeezed it. "See you later, dear."

Total silence followed her exit from the conference room.

The board meeting broke up at five o'clock. Ben shot out of his chair and headed for the elevator.

"Terri?" he called to her the second the door opened to the condo foyer. He made a quick tour dodging packing boxes to find her. When it became clear she wasn't there, he phoned her.

She'd left the voice message on her cell phone.

Frustrated, he made a beeline for the hospital. If he knew his wife, she'd been there most of the day holding Juanita's baby. To his surprise, when he questioned the nurses, none of them had seen her.

Maybe she was in her office getting settled in.

It wasn't until he discovered it empty that a sense of foreboding assailed him. He charged down the hall to John Reagan's office.

The other man's blond head lifted when Ben walked inside. "Mr. Herrick?"

"I'm looking for my wife. You haven't seen her by any chance, have you?"

"No. In fact I went over there a couple of times to ask if she needed any more help, but she wasn't there. Have you tried the hospital? She was pretty worried about that woman who had the baby."

Hell. Ben didn't need the other man to tell him what he already knew about his wife!

"Thanks for the suggestion," he bit out.

"Sure."

Terri could be in a hundred different places. There was no help for it but to have an all call put out over the PA system from the chief purser's office. Ben rang Jose and told him what he wanted him to do.

In a minute the message went out through the entire ship for Mrs. Herrick to get in touch with her husband. The only thing to do now was to go back to the condo and wait for her to either call or show up.

On his way to the elevator his cell phone rang. He clicked on. "Terri?"

"Sorry, Mr. Herrick. This is Les Cramer on the flight deck. I heard your all call. Your wife took a flight out of here at noon today."

Ben's heart almost stopped beating. "In *this* weather?"

"It wasn't as bad earlier. I assumed you knew. The pilot wouldn't have taken her up if there'd been any hint of risk. She said she was in a hurry to get back to Guayaquil, that it was an emergency."

Lord. "What was his flight plan?"

"He flew to El Cerita. Depending on the weather, he'd either go all the way to Guayaquil, or stay put till it was safe to fly."

"Has he checked in with you yet?"

"No, but I can still reach him."

"Do it now while I'm on the line, then patch me through to him!"

"Yes, sir."

Like his near-drowning experience where his life flashed before him, images of Terri flooded Ben's mind and heart till he couldn't breathe. If anything happened to her…

"Mr. Herrick? I've got Jim Nash on the line. Go ahead."

"Jim?"

"Yes, Mr. Herrick." The pilot sounded far away. There was a lot of static.

"Are you still in La Cerita?"

"Yes, sir. I've just made the decision to stay over until tomorrow. Your wife took a taxi to the Hotel Flores."

"Thank God. Both of you stay put until further notice."

"Yes, sir."

"Les?"

"I'm here."

"I need your best pilot to fly me to the nearest airport from the ship."

"Just a minute. Let's see… You could probably make it to San Cristobal."

"That's fine. I'll drive from there to La Cerita. I'm on my way up. Tell the pilot to get ready."

"Yes, sir."

The pilot had told Terri La Cerita was a small town of thirty thousand people. He made arrangements for them to stay at the Hotel Flores, which catered to American tourists. They would both be comfortable there.

Jim Nash had been terrific to her, but when she'd begged him to fly her the rest of the way, he'd adamantly refused. After putting her in a taxi, he told her he'd check in at the hotel later. That was hours ago.

She ate dinner by herself in the restaurant, watching for him in case he felt like joining her. When he didn't come, she went back to her room and got ready for bed, presuming she wouldn't hear from him until morning.

Thank heaven there'd been a way to get off the ship. After that dreadful experience in the boardroom, she couldn't have faced Ben again. The pain would have been too immobilizing.

As soon as she arrived in Lead, she would take steps to get their marriage annulled. When she thought about it, their relationship wasn't that different from two ships passing in the night.

For a short period they'd felt a mystical connection. Two mortals reaching out to each other for comfort in a dark sea. But that temporary assuagement was as ephemeral as the night itself. With the advent of morning, they'd found themselves at opposite points of the compass, out of sight, out of touch.

She stared down at her ringless left hand. She'd left the rings he'd given her on the dresser in the guest bedroom. Now she had nothing tangible to remind her of him. That was the way it had to be, she couldn't bear it otherwise.

She couldn't cope with anything right now. How was she going to make it through the night, let alone the rest of her life?

Beth. I'll call Beth.

No sooner did she reach for the phone on the table than she heard a knock on the door. She got up from the bed. "Jim?"

"It's Ben. Open the door, Terri."

She froze. No— It couldn't be.

"Shall I tell the manager to unlock it because my wife is too ill to get out of bed?"

"Please don't," she begged, struggling for breath. "I'm coming."

Her body shook uncontrollably as she crossed the short distance to undo the lock and chain guard. He pushed the door open and stormed in, slamming it behind him.

Terri took a step back, scarcely recognizing this man whose emotions had gone beyond anger to something else she couldn't comprehend.

In the dim light from the bedside table his face had the gaunt, haggard look of an older man. He was breathing heavily, like someone who'd been running miles without stopping.

Gone was the sling. His ship whites were damp and wrinkled, his dark hair disheveled.

She didn't have enough moisture left in her mouth to swallow. "J-Jim said it was too dangerous to fly."

"As you can see, he was wrong." His voice grated.

In the next breath he seized her by the upper arms, bringing her close enough she could see into his eyes.

Terri gasped.

They were the same pain-filled gray eyes that had spoken to her with such frantic urgency when she'd first looked into them at the hospital. Alone and helpless, he'd tried desperately to convey something vital. She'd felt his soul reaching out to her then.

She felt it reaching out to her now.

"What is it?" she cried in an agonized whisper.

His hands tightened, but she didn't think he was aware of it. "Why did you leave the ship?"

It was truth time. Better to get it all said and end this nightmare for both of them.

Hot tears gushed from her eyes. "Because I knew you couldn't stand me anymore."

A noise escaped his throat. It sounded like ripping silk. "In the name of all that's holy, where did you ever get an idea like that?"

"Because you threw me to the wolves this morning!" She flung the words at him. "After the horrendous way I hurt you, I know I deserved it. The only thing I could think of to do was get out of your life," she said on a sob.

"*How* do you think you hurt me? Tell me!" He gave her a gentle shake.

"On our wedding night I trampled all over your beau-

tiful dream. Here you gave me everything, and I—I—''
She was so convulsed she couldn't talk.

He crushed her against his hard body. "You only said
what I've known and felt from the inception of my idea
back in high school. But when you dream dreams on that
scale, you need backers. That means compromise.

"All along I've tried to convince myself that half a loaf
was better than none. Until my adorable new bride ex-
pressed what I'd known in my own heart from the embryo
stage of my idea. Your passionate input gave me the cour-
age to try something outrageous.

"If anyone's terrified *I* am for putting you in that position this morning. I know what I did was unforgivable,
but I knew if you couldn't convince them, no one could."

Terri sniffed. She couldn't believe what she was hearing. Slowly she lifted her head. "You actually thought *I*
could accomplish what the creator couldn't?"

His eyes wandered over each feature of her upturned
face. "I once told you you're a woman who lights her own
fires. You stole into my hospital room and proceeded to
transform my life.

"On that first afternoon when you got to the part where
you told me you were divorced, my first thought was,
thank God! Because you see by then, I had already fallen
in love with you."

"You did?" Her voice squeaked for joy.

"Yes, my love. You can't imagine my guilt. There you
were, trying to find your ex-husband. And there I lay, helpless to tell you he'd died, and loving you so deeply I knew
I had to have you or nothing else in life mattered anymore.

"Make no mistake. If you hadn't let me slip that diamond ring on your finger in Lead, I would have let the
Atlantis sail without me because I wasn't going anywhere
without you."

"Oh, darling—" She threw her arms around his neck.

"I've loved you so terribly from the moment I looked into your eyes. Those beautiful eyes that reached out to me in pain and compassion. I wanted to ease your suffering. I wanted to climb on the bed next to you and hold you in my arms, comfort you.

"My guilt was so much greater, Ben. I had no idea if you had a wife or a lover. But it didn't seem to matter. I'd found the man I'd been searching for all my life. I would never have let you go. I love you more than life itself. Lov—"

His cry of joy smothered the rest of her words as his mouth hungrily covered hers. He picked her up and carried her to bed, following her nightgown-clad body down against the mattress.

"Do you have any idea how beautiful you are? How much I've been aching to make love to my precious wife? My very heart?"

Oh, yes. Terri knew. After such long suppressed passion, words weren't enough. She had to show him what he meant to her and began devouring him in earnest.

She couldn't help it. With one touch of his hands, her body exploded with desire. His mouth was driving her crazy. Entwined in his arms and legs, she'd reached a level of rapture that had set her on fire.

This was her adored husband loving her into oblivion. She had no sense of time or space. All she knew was this driving need for fulfillment with the man who'd captured her heart, body and soul.

When the phone rang, Terri groaned in displeasure. After a glorious night of lovemaking, she'd fallen asleep in her husband's arms. She couldn't bear for anything to disturb their contentment.

It kept ringing.

She felt Ben's chest rise and fall in protest before he

reached for the receiver. When he said hello, his voice sounded an octave deeper than usual. Terri loved it. She loved him. She loved everything about him.

After a minute she heard him say all right, then he hung up the receiver and promptly found her mouth as if he were starving for her. Since she'd been in that abandoned state since last night, she responded with a voracious hunger of her own, dying for the whole loving process to begin all over again and again.

They were both moaning in ecstasy when he suddenly pulled away from her and sat up.

"Darling—" she half gasped in protest and raised herself up on one elbow. "What's wrong? Is it your shoulder?"

"No, my love." He leaned down to kiss the end of her well-shaped nose. "That was Jim. He says we have a small window of opportunity to get back to the ship if we leave now. Otherwise we may have to wait another day."

"Where is your pilot?"

"In San Cristobal. I drove here."

"Oh, Ben. I always cause you so much trouble."

"Hush." He whispered the words against her mouth. "We'd better not keep Jim waiting."

It took superhuman effort, but she managed to get away from him and hurried into the shower. Ben followed, shutting them inside.

She blushed. "If you stay in here, I'm afraid we'll never come out."

His smile was wicked. "Tired of your husband already?"

"You know I'm not." Her voice trembled. Much as she wanted to stay right here and forget the world, she knew she couldn't do that. This was only the second day of the sailing. Everyone was depending on him.

"Say the word and I'll tell Jim we've decided to go into hiding for the duration."

She cupped his handsome face with its slight male rasp. "We can do that in the condo."

His eyes ignited with light. "Promise?"

"Don't you know by now I'm out of my mind in love with you?"

"Enough to have a baby with me? I could have made you pregnant last night."

"I'm hoping you did. But just to make sure, let's hurry home. We have a lot of lost time to make up for."

He pressed a kiss to her mouth. It was hot with desire. "I'll leave you alone to get ready. But I'm warning you now, when we're back at the condo, you can forget the word privacy."

"Promise?" she teased.

To her surprise, his expression grew serious.

"What is it, darling?"

"I have something to tell you."

"And?"

"I don't want it to change things between us now."

Her heart thudded in alarm. "How could anything do that?"

"Because you're not the average woman."

She blinked. "Is there something about me you don't like?"

His eyes closed tightly for a moment. "No, darling. It's just that you throw yourself into everything you do with such passion."

"I know. It's my greatest fault."

"It's not a fault. It's a gift you have. It's so powerful, you managed to convince the board they shouldn't have been so hasty in some of their decisions. In a word, you made them see the light.

"They voted to get rid of the ban on children and pets. You're now in charge of seeing about schools and day care centers. They want you to work up a new sales brochure to present at the next board meeting.''

''Ben!'' She practically shrieked in delight.

''I knew it.''

His comment brought her up short. ''What?''

He didn't say anything.

''Darling?''

''I can already see that look in your eyes.''

''What look?''

''It's the one you get when you're going after something.''

She was trying to understand. ''What does this conversation have to do with something changing in our marriage?''

He sucked in his breath. ''I'm a possessive man. I've found that I don't like sharing you. The other night when I walked in the condo and you had dinner ready for me, I thought I'd died and gone to heaven.''

''That's never going to change. I'm your wife first and always.''

''You say that now…''

''Now and forever,'' she declared, stunned by his vulnerability. Who would have guessed? ''You think I like being separated from you? I have an idea that will solve our problem. Why don't I move the chamber of commerce into your office. We'll work together.'' There was fire in her eye as she said, ''That way we'll be able to coordinate all our coffee breaks, long lunches and early dinners.''

He pulled her back in his arms. ''As long as it means we spend them in each other's arms, you have my blessing. I love you, Terri,'' he cried as the phone rang again. A reminder that they were going home where they belonged.

Genoa, Italy.

Ben checked his watch. It was ten after five in the evening. He threw down his pen, unable to work at his desk any longer. Feeling at a loose end, he got up from the chair and left his office for the condo.

For the last couple of hours he'd expected Terri to come walking through the doors of their combined office, excited to tell him about her shopping spree.

Earlier in the day she'd gone ashore in one of the tenders with Juanita. They'd decided to pick out some more things for the new day care center Juanita was running with two other licensed day care specialists.

According to Terri, the Italians made the best children's toys. She wanted to check them out and thought Juanita could use a few hours away from the demands of little Rosita, and her job. Now that all the condos were sold, the center was always filled with small children.

He didn't like it when Terri was away from him. Hell. He missed her like the devil. Everything fell flat without the wife he adored. She'd promised they'd only be gone part of the day, but he should have realized she'd get engrossed and lose track of the time. What surprised him was that she hadn't phoned yet.

While the *Atlantis* was in this part of the Mediterranean for the next few weeks, he planned to take her to Venice and Florence for a surprise on-shore honeymoon. Tomorrow was their four month anniversary.

After breakfast in the morning they would leave the ship. He had a rental car waiting. They would find a charming pensione in the hills of Tuscany and lose themselves in each other for days and nights on end. He might let her out long enough to do a little sightseeing, but he wasn't making any promises. Her loving brought him alive. As far as he knew, she felt the same way about him.

Would it be enough if he couldn't give her children? Or if she couldn't carry a child to full term?

He'd purposely left that subject alone. It was more important to him that they enjoy their honeymoonlike marriage without any pressure that might take away from their joy. When he felt the time was right, he'd talk to her about it. After this side trip was over, he'd get her a new puppy. She was partial to little Pugs.

The second the elevator opened to the foyer he called out to her, hoping to hear her voice. When silence greeted his ears, his disappointment was greater than he could believe.

He headed for the bedroom to shower and change. If she still hadn't returned by then, he would make dinner to surprise her. But his footsteps stilled when he saw that their bedroom door was closed. There was a sign taped to it.

Stop. Go to the guest bedroom and prepare yourself. You'll find the necessary clothing on the bed. When you're ready, knock on this door three times.

Ben would have laughed, but excitement had already started to sweep through him like an F-5 tornado. He swore his adorable wife was going to give him a heart attack one of these days.

Prepare myself.

He chuckled inwardly as he showered in the guest bathroom. But by the time he'd donned the new beige silk robe with an Egyptian motif of all things, his amusement had changed to desire that was building in quantum leaps.

When he stood at the door, his hand trembled harder with each knock.

"Go away unless you are my body servant Orastes."

Orastes?

"This is the night I celebrate the blessing of life. Only Orastes is permitted the pleasure of my company."

Suddenly something clicked in his brain.

"It is I, Orastes, your highness."

"How do I know this is not a trick?"

"You have heard my voice many times before, oh fair one. I live only to serve you."

"You may enter."

The moment he stepped inside, it was like he'd gone back in time. The room had been transformed down to the temptress on the bed swathed in some flowing white creation right out of Pharaoh's court. Her eyes, outlined in black, glowed like great blue jewels.

"Come here, my love." She held out her arms to him. "I have a gift for you. Then we will embrace one last time before Pharaoh's guards discover us."

His wife was the most exciting woman he'd ever known, but tonight she'd outdone herself. He knew this was all playacting, but there was something mysterious and provocative about her right now.

It was almost as if she really were the wife of Pharaoh and he was the besotted guard who'd been forced to undergo live mummification for the crime of daring to love her.

"Orastes—" She beckoned him with unfeigned longing.

He joined her on the bed, wanting to crush her voluptuous red mouth beneath his. But she thrust a small package in his hands, preventing him from taking what was undeniably his.

"Open this quickly."

Aroused by her witchery, his fingers were all thumbs as he removed the wrapping.

He blinked. After being caught up in the ancient past, it took him a moment to recognize the early pregnancy test device for what it was. There was a red line matching the other one.

Their eyes fused.

"Darling—" he cried before searching blindly for her mouth. Then they were clinging to each other as if it really were their last moment on earth.

"My love," he whispered as he kissed her face and neck feverishly. "I've wanted this for so long." He lifted his head so he could look into her eyes again. "I'm going to take such perfect care of you, nothing will happen to our child."

Her eyes glistened with tears. "I know it won't. You see, I'm already past my first trimester."

"What?"

She nodded. "I'm fifteen weeks pregnant already. The ship's obstetrician doesn't foresee any problems. That's because I'm married to the most wonderful husband alive."

"Terri— You kept this from me all this time?"

"Please don't be hurt."

"I'm not. I'm so happy, I think I'm in shock."

"You never noticed certain changes?"

He flashed her a wicked smile. "Now that I think about it, yes."

"You thought I'd been gaining weight."

"In all the right places," he murmured against her mouth before devouring it. "When I walked in here a few minutes ago, I thought I'd never seen you looking more beautiful."

Her seductive eyes narrowed like a cat's. "I'm the luckiest of women to be pregnant by my handsome husband. Quick now. Embrace me one more time. The guards are on their way up with a special dinner prepared by your favorite chef."

"Now?" He groaned.

"I'm afraid so. Ship gossip tells me he's made this fabulous cake for the new father-to-be. But don't worry, darling." She pulled him as close as she possibly could.

"After he leaves, destiny has decreed our love will go on, and on, and on, and on. If you don't believe me, I know a certain video we can watch…"